Western   Bishop, Bill.   FEB 0
BISHOP
Bill   Two Hearts.

WITHDRAWN   S0-CAS-761

Two Hearts

B 0 1 2020

IWM

Two Hearts

The Tale of Cole Younger's Sweetheart:
A Barton Family Saga

BILL BISHOP

RESOURCE *Publications* · Eugene, Oregon

TWO HEARTS
The Tale of Cole Younger's Sweetheart: A Barton Family Saga

Copyright © 2019 Bill Bishop. All rights reserved. Except for brief quotations in critical publications or reviews, no part of this book may be reproduced in any manner without prior written permission from the publisher. Write: Permissions, Wipf and Stock Publishers, 199 W. 8th Ave., Suite 3, Eugene, OR 97401.

Resource Publications
An Imprint of Wipf and Stock Publishers
199 W. 8th Ave., Suite 3
Eugene, OR 97401

www.wipfandstock.com

PAPERBACK ISBN: 978-1-5326-7730-4
HARDCOVER ISBN: 978-1-5326-7731-1
EBOOK ISBN: 978-1-5326-7732-8

Manufactured in the U.S.A.   JULY 12, 2019

This book is dedicated
to my mother,
Velda Bishop, a true pioneer
and
to my wife, Izumi, who
somehow puts up with me

Contents

Acknowledgments

THERE ARE ALWAYS PEOPLE to thank in any endeavor. I would like to thank my mother, Velda Bishop, for telling and retelling the Barton family myth about Cole Younger's sweetheart since my childhood. Though my version of events differs from the sketchy facts surrounding the Barton family myth, I have tried to stay true to the basic story.

I would like to thank my brothers, Daniel and Daryl Bishop, for taking the time to proofread an early draft of this story and for correcting my many typos and providing valuable advice. I would like to especially thank my cousin Randall Barton whose early frank critique and feedback helped me see the need to better flesh out my "cardboard characters" and tighten up the overall story.

This early feedback and advice helped me to work out some of the story's kinks and to better flesh out the characters which greatly improved the final manuscript.

Preface

THE GENESIS OF THIS novel is a Barton family myth that has been passed down through the generations for more than 140 years. As the story goes, the Barton brothers rode with the James brothers after the Civil War. During these outlaw days, my great-great grandfather ran off with Cole Younger's sweetheart. It has been further claimed that she may have been part Seneca or Cherokee Indian. As the tale has been told, the couple first met along a small river in northwest Missouri where she was doing laundry. They fell in love, later ran off, got married, and had children who continued the Barton family march west into the Dakota Territory and beyond.

The hero of the tale as I have tried to reconstruct events is Bill Barton who was born in Illinois in 1845 to Amorett Waite and Oromal Bingham Barton. Bill Barton moved from Illinois to Iowa shortly after the Civil War in 1865. John Barton, Bill Barton's oldest son, was born in Iowa in 1868. John married in Iowa in 1897 and had seven children—three sons and four daughters—and later homesteaded at Rainy Creek near the little town of Creighton, Pennington County in western South Dakota in 1912. John's oldest son, Bill Barton, named for his grandfather, later married Kathrine (Kate) Busskohl and had three children—two sons, Harold and John, and one daughter, Velda, my mother. From 1929 until 1935, Bill and Kate Barton homesteaded the last available free land near Dewey in Custer County in the Black Hills of South Dakota not far from where gold was first discovered on French Creek in 1874.

I have spun both fact and fiction into this epic tale, drawing from historical facts about the Barton family as well as facts surrounding: Jesse and Frank James; Cole, Jim, Bob, and John Younger; William Quantrill; Bloody-Bill Anderson; Clell Miller; Charlie Pitts; Bill Chadwell; Belle Starr; Judge Shirley; Allen Pinkerton; General George Armstrong Custer; Capitan Leander McNelly; Dan Rice; and many others as well as drawing from the many accounts of the Northfield, Minnesota bank robbery and the ensuing manhunt. The story roughly takes place over a ten-year period from the end of the Civil War in 1865 to the presidential election in 1876.

As it happens, the year 1876 marks a watershed in American history. Many tectonic events converged during the preceding decade that have in many ways set the foundations of the America in which we live today. From the purchase of the Alaskan territory, the completion of the first transcontinental railroad, the rise of the Pinkerton National Detective Agency (later to evolve into today's FBI), the opening of the last Indian lands in the Dakotas, and the celebration of America's first centennial, to the globalization of the ice trade, the establishment of America's modern day Christmas traditions, the discovery of the telephone, the death of George Armstrong Custer at the Battle of the Little Big Horn, the demise of the James-Younger Gang in Northfield, Minnesota, and the contested presidential election of 1876 which led to the sudden decision to withdraw federal troops and end southern Reconstruction, resulting in the loss of civil rights for millions of newly freed slaves for nearly one hundred years.

All these events and many more have been woven into the story, each playing a role in helping to set the stage and propel the plot forward. In writing this fictional account, I found it necessary to include a few historical facts, believing we are all products of the times in which we live. Bill Barton and Lucy Breeden were no different.

This is a work of fiction, none of the characters or events depicted in this story are intended to represent any true persons either living or deceased or their true actions or intentions or any actual historical events. This fictional novel is at best a flight of fancy based on a long-held Barton family myth. The author's intent is to entertain, not to inform readers of the accurate recounting of historical persons, facts, or events. The author reserves the right to leave the writing of history to historians. As to those things that may be plausible, the author believes the realm of the possible is limited only by an understanding of the facts and your own imagination.

BILL BISHOP
Hot Springs, South Dakota
July 22, 2018

May 1, 1867

Lizard Creek, Webster County, Iowa

Secret Refuge

THE SKY BURNED SCARLET red as the sun set over Lizard Creek. Bill Barton tipped back in his rocker as he took a deep pull on his pipe, causing sparks to flare up in its corncob bowl. He blew out a large plume of smoke that drifted off into the dimming light of the evening carried by a gentle breeze. It was a good life here in Webster County, Iowa, and Bill had finally found peace.

Bill Barton was a tall man with broad shoulders and a trim build. His jet-black wavy hair cropped above his collar framed a chiseled face with high cheekbones that had been battle-hardened after five long years of war. His deep hazel blue eyes shined with the intelligence of an inquisitive mind. He had fought for the victorious Union Army only to come home to Camp Point in Adams County, Illinois, to find that his father, mother, and younger siblings had all died during a typhus outbreak and that the family farm was in the hands of the local bank. Broke and brokenhearted, Bill had drifted west in search of a new life.

He was happy his cousin Wilber Waite on his mother's side had looked him up after the war. Wilber and his wife Nancy followed Bill west to Iowa, settling a place nearby and quickly filling it up with more kids than Bill could keep track of. Wilber, ever grateful for all the help Bill had given him after the war, was always willing to watch Bill's place while he was away on frequent business dealings in Missouri. Bill had not shared any details about his business in war-torn Missouri, knowing Wilber, a God-fearing man, would not have approved. Wilber simply would never condone out-law ways nor believe that his cousin was one.

Driven by his desire to right the wrongs of the past, Bill had poured himself, body and soul, into getting back what he had lost. He worked day and night to hone out of the wilderness a new place, one built with his own two hands, his strong back, the sweat of his brow, and the livestock stolen from southern men—men who had taken his family from him and every-thing he had held dear. Bill still had a herd of rustled cattle being held in the sprawling stockyards in Kansas City that he needed to sell and sell quickly. He knew the stockyard fees to feed and water his herd of five hundred head of cattle were literally eating up his profits by the day. He also worried that the rightful owner of the herd might just check those stockyard pens before he could get the herd sold and moved on east. He needed to make a trip to Westport where a buyer from St. Louis had agreed to meet him in just two days. He would have to leave at daybreak the next morning.

Though the odds were no better than fifty-fifty whether he would be met by the law or by a smiling cattle buyer with cash in hand, he had no choice but to roll the dice. If he pulled this deal off, he had told himself it might be a good time to put his outlaw days behind him. Despite his mixed feelings about giving up his outlaw life, he had become increasingly concerned about his forays into Missouri and further south. Over the past couple of years since the end of the war, cattle rustling had gotten a damn sight riskier and more dangerous by the day as law enforcement became more and more organized. What concerned him even more was that his old rustling buddies in Missouri had become hardened gunslinging outlaws. He never wanted any of these ruthless killers to ever find out who he really was or where he lived. His place on Lizard Creek south of Fort Dodge had become his refuge, his dream come true. He needed to guard its secret and that of his true identity when south of the Mason-Dixon, or the promise of his new life would end in death like his old life had back in Illinois.

The next morning, Wilber rode into Bill's place at first light. Wilber was a big-boned man who always had a good word and a smile on his face. As Wilber's horse cleared the gate, Bill was standing in front of his house, tightening the cinch on his saddle. Turning in the direction of the approaching hoofbeats, Bill's big jet-black Morgan made a low whinny, and Wilber's bay-colored Appaloosa snorted in reply.

"Mornin' Wilber. I didn't think I'd see you up and around this early in the mornin," Bill said as he looked up from his work.

"Mornin' partner," Wilber said as he stepped down from his horse.

"No need seein' me off," Bill said as he secured the straps on his bedroll and saddlebags. "This trip'll be a short one. I should be back in a week or so."

"Good, good," Wilber said, as though not really listening. "I have a sick cow I've been tending to and she had me up all night," Wilber continued, kicking at a dirt clod. "Thought I might as well swing by to see you off."

"How are Nancy and the little ones?" Bill said with a knowing grin. He figured Wilber had a hell of a lot more on his mind than a sick cow.

"Everyone's fine, just fine," Wilber said flatly as he met Bill's grin. "Oh, and Nancy is expecting again. I guess we'll soon be adding to the herd," he continued, looking sideways at Bill and matching his knowing grin.

"I swear, Wilber, you and Nancy seem to be on a mission to fill the wild west with little Waites from one end to the other," Bill said with a chuckle.

"Heck Bill, this is only our fourth," Wilber said dryly. "We plan to have at least ten, possibly a full dozen. Hell, we may even make it a baker's dozen, though it might not be lucky to stop at thirteen." With that Bill and Wilber shared a good-natured laugh.

After checking all the straps securing his gear one last time, Bill swung up on his horse and settled in for a long ride. "I appreciate you keepin' an eye on things," Bill said. "I'll bring back some sweets for Nancy and the kids from Kansas City. May need to buy a pack mule to tote all the goodies back if you keep adding more stock to your herd," he added with a chuckle and a wink.

"Good to hear you'll be gone only a week or so. Things'll be busier on my place before long," Wilber said. "You never know, Bill; your bachelor days may be numbered. Might be time for you to round up a cute little heifer and start your own herd. A guy never knows when some little sweet thing might run off with his heart."

"No worries on me rounding up a little heifer on this trip, Wilber," Bill said with a smile. "You can tell Nancy she can continue her efforts to get me hitched when I get back."

Wilber's wife had never let a Sunday pass without offering to introduce Bill to a prospective bride. Bill was an eligible bachelor with land, a strong back, and plenty of promise. Nancy believed a man needed to build a strong family, one that would endure long after he passed. She was determined to get Bill started as soon as possible. Try as she might, finding a good woman, getting married, starting a family, and filling a house up with a bunch of bawling kids were the furthest things from Bill's mind. A devout bachelor, Bill could never understand why Wilber had gotten married so young or why he and Nancy wanted to have so many damn children. Giving Wilber a final tip of the hat, Bill rode out, leaving Lizard Creek behind him.

Bill and Wilber, like all frontier pioneers, knew how to predict the weather by reading nature's signs. Learning to predict weather events was a matter of survival for those who lived off the land. They also shared many common superstitions of the day, from knocking on wood to throwing a pinch of salt over their left shoulders. Wilber being a religious man, however, had always placed his faith in God: what happened was God's will. Though Bill believed in God's will, he also believed there were ways to predict the outcome of things. He had been taught by his grandfather that seemingly natural events often hold deeper meanings that can be read. He had learned many of these during his boyhood days in Illinois. Like his grandfather, Bill believed he could spot these signs and divine their meanings.

As he rode out of Webster County, Wilber's parting words seemed to echo off something deep in Bill's mind: "A guy never knows when some little sweet thing might run off with his heart." On reflection he could only shrug, knowing that what the future held only the wind knew. Looking up, he noticed a flock of birds circling above him, and then carried by the wind, headed southwest. Taking this sign as a good omen, he turned southwest and urged his horse to pick up the pace.

May 2, 1867

Little Platte River, Buchanan County, Missouri

Love at First Blush

BILL RODE SOUTHWEST ACROSS the north branch of the Raccoon River and down between the Tarkio and Nodaway Rivers crossing the state line just north of the little town of Tarkio in Atchison County, Missouri. He then steered clear of the larger towns of Maryville, Savana, and St. Joseph until he reached the Little Platte River that ran down through Buchanan and Platte countries. This was a familiar route he had taken many times when he rode in and out of Missouri on cattle rustling forays.

Bill normally waited until he reached the crossing at Independence on the Missouri River to rest up; however, the unseasonable heat convinced him it wouldn't hurt to stop awhile to stretch his legs and water his horse. He was thirsty, and he was sure his horse was as well. It was getting late in the day and he knew he wouldn't reach Kansas City before sunset. His plan was to find a place to stay in Independence, a busy port town on the Missouri River where a lone rider wouldn't arouse a second look.

Plunging his horse through the low-lying bushes that separated the Little Platte River from the main trail, Bill suddenly realized there was somebody crouching at the riverbank right in front of him. He quickly reined up his horse and slid to a stop.

"Whoa, whoa there, big guy," Bill said to his horse as he pulled up hard on the reins with one hand while leaning forward and patted his horse's neck with the other to sooth the animal's skittish nature.

Getting his horse under control, he turned his attention to the woman he now found crouching in front of him. "Howdy, sorry to startle you like

5

that, ma'am," Bill said as he swung down off his horse to let it drink. "I didn't see anyone along the river when I cut down through the brush to water my horse."

"No, no. No problem, I heard you coming before you broke through the brush. Riders often use the low river bank along here to water their horses," she said seemingly without fear. "You're not from these parts. Are you just riding through?" she continued.

Though she made no move, Bill noticed her take a quick glance at the Henry repeater rifle laying not a foot from where she knelt on her knees on a large flat rock near the water's edge.

"No, I'm from up yonder in Iowa. I'm headed to Westport. I heard they're putting wagon trains together to head west. Thought I might look for a job," Bill lied as he tried to sound nonchalant though unable to take his eyes off the precious vision of beauty he had stumbled upon.

Her hair was dark black with delicate highlights of dark brown that caught the sunlight as it filtered through the leaves overhead. Her face was a perfectly symmetrical oval with high cheek bones and a proud but delicate nose, her nostrils like tiny seashells. Her lips were full and inviting. Her brow and eyebrows balanced in perfect harmony with her large and intelligent chestnut-colored eyes which missed nothing, though retaining their soft and mysterious feminine allure. Her northern European roots dominated her overall appearance; her slightly darker skin tone and hints of native influences in her features spoke of a richer heritage. Everything about her womanly shape, how she moved, the seeming lightness of her touch captivated Bill in ways he had never felt before. He could feel cold sweat run down his spine as his stomach tightened into a hard, twisted knot.

She acted nonchalant as she continued to scrub her laundry on the flat rock, only briefly looking up to speak. "It'll be dark soon, do you plan to ride on or stay the night?" she asked, seemingly without being in full control of her own mouth. She regretted her words and wondered why she asked such a question of a complete stranger. Yet she knew her heart desperately wanted to know the answer.

"Thought I might spend the night before riding on in," Bill blurted without thinking. Catching himself, he realized he knew of no place to stay in the area. "You happen to know of a good place to stay around these parts?" he asked, holding his arms out wide and rotating them in a broad arc. Having ridden through the area many times, he knew very well there wasn't a town or even a hamlet of any size within miles from where they stood.

Embarrassed, Lucy motioned with an outstretched arm. "Up the trail a way is a shack in the woods. Local folks call it Molly B's Inn," she said. "It's run by Molly B, an ol' battleax who puts up riders for the night from time to time. She's spread word far and wide around these parts that she'll put up a rider for six bits a night for grub and a bed. Can't vouch for the quality though," she added, her last words delivered in deadpan voice with a visible smirk on her face.

"Sounds like one hell of a deal. Sold!" Bill said, much too enthusiastically, and wondered if she had noticed how desperate he was to learn more about her. "You be around here tomorrow mornin'? If so, I'd like to see you again before I set out for Westport," he bravely ventured in a voice barely audible.

"No need for that. I'm sure you wouldn't want to delay an early start for Westport just to see me again," she said, her voice trailing off into no more than a whisper.

"No problem, I have all day to get to Westport tomorrow. I just like talkin' to you so much, I thought we could swap a few stories before I head out tomorrow," Bill replied, quickly praying she would agree, though not sure how a second meeting might go considering he was not much of a storyteller, at least not the kind of stories a young lady would like to hear.

"Alright, let's meet here tomorrow morning just after sun up," she said, surprising herself again with her forwardness. She too wondered what possible stories she might have to share with this stranger.

"Alri . . . ! Ah . . . that would be nice. I look forward to seeing you again just after sunrise at this here very same rock tomorrow mornin'," Bill said, unable to contain his excitement while trying to appear calm.

With a goofy smile on his face, Bill continued, "By the way, my name is Bill, Bill Barton. Glad to meet ya, ma'am. What's your name?" Bill didn't know why he had told her his real name. Since his days as a Union spy during the war, he had always used an alias when he was south of the Mason-Dixon. All he knew was that he wanted to be himself with her and not to pretend to be anyone else. He never wanted Lucy to find out he used an alias to hide his identity when in the South or that he was a cattle rustler, a horse thief, and a good-for-nothing outlaw.

"Glad to meet you, sir. My name is Lucy, Lucy Breeden," she said with a shallow curtsy. "Until tomorrow morning then. I too look forward to meetin' you again and swappin' stories," she said matter-of-factly. Inside, she hoped her cheeks were not as red as they felt because her pounding heart told her they must be ablaze in scarlet hue.

Bill gave her a slight bow and quickly mounted his horse. Smiling, he tipped his hat as he spurred his stallion up through the brush and back onto the main trail. Without looking back, though desperately wanting to, he rode straight to Molly B's Inn.

After Bill's horse slid through the brush and back onto the main trail, Lucy listened as he rode way. Finding herself alone again, she was left to wonder what had just happened. As if she had been possessed by unknown spirits, a demon named Bill Barton with a flashing white-toothed smile and piercing blue eyes had busted into her world and turned it upside down. He had gone as quickly as he had come. Every part of his handsome face smiling as he tipped his hat farewell. The thought of him brought goosebumps running down her neck and across her shoulders and arms. When their eyes first met, her eyes had reached into his soul and found a union deeper than any she had ever felt before. She was certain he felt the same about her.

But what of this stranger? Where had he come from? Who was he really? Where would a relationship with him lead the two of them? And most terrifyingly, what about Cole Younger, an outlaw who longed to possess her for himself no matter the cost in blood and treasure? How could she ever break free to follow her own heart? How could she ask this stranger to risk his life for her? Her mind heavy with unanswered questions, she finished up her chores. Wondering why she had agreed to meet again the next morning with the demon named Bill Barton, she made her way home to a sleepless night.

It wasn't until he had reached the shack in the woods that it hit him like a ton of bricks that the pretty little gal he just met and agreed to meet again tomorrow morning was none other than Lucy Breeden, the beautiful young woman with traces of Indian blood he had heard so much about who lived in these parts. There was no doubt, she was the very same so-called Cherokee Indian princess that was widely known to be Cole Younger's sweetheart. Reining up his horse in front of the shack and without getting off, Bill weighed his options. He knew right then his wisest option was to ride like hell and not look back until he reached Independence; he also knew deep down that he couldn't wait until tomorrow morning to see Lucy Breeden again. When he finally made his decision, he knew without a doubt that when it came to a choice between being with Lucy and anything else, from this day forward he would choose Lucy every time. Whether she knew it now or not, she owned his heart, and as far as he was concerned, she always would.

Just as Bill moved to dismount and before his feet could hit the ground, Molly B charged out of her shack and onto its dilapidated front porch toting a double-barreled shotgun which she quickly pointed directly at Bill's head. "Whoa there, not so fast, stranger," she barked. "Now, slowly ease off that pony and keep your hands where I can see 'em. B'fore I decide to let ya hang around, tell me clear now if'n you're one of them James-Younger varmints," she growled. "I don't cotton much to that mangy bunch of outlaws. If you're one of them, you best get back up on your hoss and ride on out of here, no harm done."

"No, ma'am. I am not part of the James-Younger Gang, I wouldn't know 'em if I met 'em," Bill said flatly. "I'm just passin' through from north of here on the way to Westport. Thought I might rest up tonight before headin' on in," he continued.

Seeing the expression on Molly B's face soften, Bill was relieved when he felt the tension between them wind down as the shotgun's double barrels slowly drifted off to one side.

"Got a name?" she barked, still holding the shotgun high.

"Name's Leroy Thompson, ma'am. I heard from some local folks that your name is Molly B," Bill said with the best kindly stranger smile he could muster.

Bill had used the name Leroy Thompson when working undercover in the South as a Union spy. The character Leroy Thompson was a southerner with a history and known to be a bit of a rogue in the border states and in many parts of the South. Bill decided to keep the identity alive after the war to provide his shadier business activities with the cover he needed. He prayed no one would ever discover that Leroy Thompson was really Bill Barton of Lizard Creek, Iowa.

As flies swarmed around a nearby outhouse, Molly B eyed him for a moment, looking him up and down with a cockeye that seemed to have a life of its own. Shrugging her massive shoulders, she lowered her shotgun. "Well then, howdy Leroy, so I take it you're lookin' for a place to hole up for the night. The Molly B Inn has the best grub this side of the Mississip'. Leastwise, that's what all my payin' guests tell me," Molly B boomed in a manly voice followed by a high-pitched cackle.

Molly B was a mountain of a woman, as big around as she was tall. She wore men's buckskin pants and shirt and had broad lumberjack shoulders with arms covered in thick cords of muscle. That she also had no lack of facial hair was a fact hard not to miss. She was a manly woman you might say, but only to yourself if you wanted to remain in the land of the living. It was mighty clear to Bill that Molly B didn't take guff from anyone, least of all from any mangy male varmints.

"Sounds mighty fine to me, ma'am, I'd like to try that famous grub and stay the night. I'll be riding out at first light tomorrow mornin'," Bill said, maintaining the broad smile he had affixed to his face.

"That'll be six bits for supper, a bed, and breakfast in the mornin'. Another two bits to feed and water your hoss," Molly said.

"A fair price, a buck for the night. Where can I put up my horse? I'd like to let him roll and then rub him down before nightfall," Bill said, looking the place over.

"The barn shed is just around back, you can put him up there. There ain't no oats but there's plenty of hay and water there for him. Supper's at six o'clock sharp, don't be late," she said, and with that she turned quickly and marched back into the shack.

Bill entered the dimly lit shack after rubbing down his horse. Molly B, standing at the stove, held a large ladle in her right hand which she used to point out his bunk for the night and a wash basin with a crumpled towel next to it. Bill had no more than stowed his gear and washed up when, without ceremony, supper was slapped on the table.

"Come 'n get it!" Molly B bellowed as she swung her substantial girth into the larger of the two chairs at the table.

Bill took up his chair in front of a steaming bowl of mystery stew and what he soon discovered were rock-hard sourdough biscuits. As he surveyed his meal, Molly B wasted no time digging in.

"Well, Leroy. This your first time in these parts?" Molly B asked between loud slurping and smacking sounds that followed every spoon-full of stew she shoved into her whisker-ringed mouth.

"No, I've ridden through before but never stayed the night," he replied, not wanting to stray too far from the truth. He had learned long ago that if you are going to lie, you need to stick to the truth as much as possible.

During his years as a Union spy, the maxim he had lived by was: It is better to spin a fresh version of the truth than to attempt to make up everything from whole cloth. When cornered, he had always found it was easier to remember a few twisted facts and a lie or two than the many details of a make-believe life.

Their conversation stayed on the light side, with Molly B more interesting in wolfing down her food than conversing with her guest. Though Bill was relieved not to have to maintain a conversation, he struggled, bite by miserable bite, to clean up his stew and biscuits. After supper, Bill retired to the porch where he found an old rocker. Much like he had done the evening before back in Lizard Creek, he watched the sun slowly slide behind the horizon while smoking his corncob pipe. Unlike the evening before, he couldn't get Wilber's final words out of his mind, "A guy never knows when some little sweet thing might run off with his heart."

He felt something had happen at the Little Platte, something he couldn't quite explain. He knew Lucy must have also felt it. Whatever it was, he was convinced Lucy was the "little sweet thing" that had indeed run off with his heart.

Returning indoors, Bill found Molly B busy cleaning her shotgun and several rifles she had laid out on her bed. Following her lead, Bill squatted on a stool next his bunk and cleaned and oiled his Winchester rifle and Colt pistol. It didn't take Bill long to notice that Molly B had been drinking while he was outside on the porch; not only were her cheeks clearly flushed, she had become considerably more talkative.

Molly B talked of her desire to head up to Washington Territory to join up with some of her kinfolk as soon as she had a big enough grubstake. She worried that the territory might become a state before she got there, considering Oregon had already become a state in 1859 before the war. Now that the war was over, news of a surge in wagon trains headed west filled the newspapers.

Recent news reports that President Andrew Johnson had purchased a huge new territory further north on the west coast called Alaska from Russia had grabbed Molly B's imagination. She was convinced the new territory held even more treasures, from furs to gold and possibly much, much more than any of the others.

"If'n Washington Territory is gettin' too crowded, we might just head north to Alaska to strike it rich. Hell, we might even put a dancing polar bear act together for Dan Rice's Greatest Show, now wouldn't that be a hoot," she blubbered as she leaned heavily on the edge of her bed, her cock-eye only half open. Looking over at Bill, she gave him a whisker-rimmed gap-tooth grin and then let out a godawful giggle. It was clear to Bill the alcohol was working its magic.

Dan Rice's Greatest Show was one the most widely known circuses in the country during and after the Civil War. Nearly everyone in the country knew or had heard about the circus performer, clown, and comedian Dan Rice. Dan had performed in both the North and the South during the war from 1861 through 1865 leading many to wonder which side he supported. After the war, he continued to put on shows and provided financial assistance to people impacted by the war in both the North and the South. Attempting to leverage his national notoriety, Dan Rice would make a failed bid for the presidency in 1868.

Bill had read about the Alaska treaty negotiations that had only just concluded on March 30, 1867 with the purchase price for the territory set at $7,200,000, or about two cents per acre. Though the purchase had been dubbed Steward's Folly after Secretary of State William Steward, who had conducted the negotiations, Bill agreed with Molly B, as did most newspapers, that the deal was the steal of the century and that with the possible annexation of British Columbia—also mentioned in the news—it would greatly expand America's domination of the entire North American continent. The promise of a prosperous future for the nation made Bill feel proud. He hoped that one day his children would play a role in building that nation.

Bill surprised himself with such a thought. It was the first time in his life he had ever seriously pondered having children or of what mark they might make in the future. He suspected that thoughts of Lucy which had run through his mind for hours had started to carve new channels of thought. Thoughts he had never really considered until now. He desperately hoped that Lucy's mind was also being etched with new channels of thought about him and their future together.

Quite unexpectedly, no more than an hour after sunset, Molly B doused the lanterns and without further word went to bed. Suddenly finding himself in the dark, Bill was left to grope around until finally settling into his bunk for the night. Rather than quickly falling asleep as was his custom, he found himself tossing and turning, unable to stop thinking about anything but seeing the beautiful Lucy Breeden again. Molly B's incessant snoring that reverberated through every board and timber in the little shack rattled every bone in his body. It was the kind of lullaby that did little to help a man sleep. Unable to stop thinking about Lucy while fighting to hold down a supper that seemed to have a mind of its own, it wasn't until the wee hours of the morning that Bill finally gave in to utter exhaustion and fell into a deep sleep.

May 3, 1867

Little Platte River, Buchanan County, Missouri

Beating as One

MOLLY B WAS UP before sunrise. The banging of pots and pans brought Bill back to the land of the living not two hours after he had finally fallen asleep. Bill had no more than pulled on his clothes and finished throwing a little water on his face from the dirty wash basin next to his bunk when, without much formality, breakfast was served.

"Well now, how'd ya'll sleep last night?" Molly asked, tilting her head to one side, making her cockeye bug out in an alarming way. "Ya know, that fine bed over there came all the way up the muddy Mo from St. Louie," she continued, pointing at the sad-looking, swaybacked bunk in the corner he had just crawled out of.

"Slept like a stone," Bill lied. "Good thing I stopped here to rest up before my ride into Westport," he added, looking down at the breakfast spread out before him. His plate had been piled under with burnt beans and eggs that looked more fit for a hog trough than any payin' guest. His stomach groaned as he scooped up a heap of beans and took his first bite.

Conversation again stayed light, though Molly B was more than a little curious about who might have told Bill about Molly B's Inn. Bill had pretended not to remember exactly who told him, saying he thought it was some old farmer he had met on the trail. Molly B seemed to doubt his story but didn't challenge him about it.

Molly B was also interested in news about the latest James-Younger Gang escapades. She seemed particularly interested in Cole Younger. Her interest in the gang seemed odd to Bill considering her stated distain for the whole mangy bunch just the day before. More than once she asked him if he knew Cole Younger or if he had ever met him. She said Cole might even be in Buchanan County and hinted that he often rode along the Little Platte. She also spoke of a certain Indian maiden who often did laundry along the Little Platte just up the trail not far from her place and how it was widely known Cole was sweet on the little gal.

"You sure you didn't see a little red-skinned honey down by the Little Platte on your way here?" Molly B probed as she studied Bill's reaction. "Like I said, that little Indian princess is a sweet one and Cole Younger would kill any man who tried to lay his hands where they weren't welcome. If'n you get my meanin'," she continued, her cockeye never blinking.

Stone-faced, Bill withstood her interrogation. He assured Molly B he hadn't seen anyone along the river when he rode through. Though Molly B clearly seemed unconvinced, she let it slide. When Bill asked her why she wanted to know so much about Cole's whereabouts, she dodged the question and shifted the conversation to all the news coming out of Kansas City.

With the booming growth of the railroads, Kansas City had grown rapidly, eclipsing Westport and even Independence to become one of the frontier's main commercial hubs. Believing Bill was headed to Westport to look for work on a wagon train, Molly B asked how long the wagon trains would continue to roll west. She was worried that the days of the wagons might be numbered. According to the newspapers, a trip from New York to San Francisco would take only seven days when the transcontinental railroad was completed in 1869, only a couple of years off.

Bill reminded Molly B that train fares would remain steep for some time, especially if you wanted to take anything with you beyond a small bag and the clothes on your back. Bill had assured Molly B the wagon trains would continue to roll as long as there was land for the taking and the promise of a new life in the northwest or the northern plains. Molly B had been pleased to hear that the wagons would continue to roll at least for the foreseeable future. Unknown to the two of them at the time, the wagon trains would continue to roll well into the 1880s until the final slaughter of the buffalo herds, the defeat and relocation of the Indian tribes, and the establishment of rail networks throughout the untamed regions.

Bill knew Molly B wanted to travel further west. She had shared her plans to join a wagon train to Washington Territory the night before. She had also hinted she had found a surefire way of building up her grubstake and that she might even be able to strike out in a year or so. Bill wondered how Molly B could build a grubstake of any size by putting up occasional guests for a buck a night. When Bill took his horse to the barn shed the night before, he had taken a close look around Molly B's place. He had noted she had no livestock to speak of and didn't seem to be a serious trapper, considering he had found no sign of hides or pelts being worked. When he added everything up, he arrived at the obvious conclusion: the income for ol' Molly B's growing grubstake was coming from somewhere on the other side of the law. Considering everything she had said, he wondered how Cole Younger might factor into her growing grubstake.

Bill ate quickly and soon saddled up. As he mounted his horse, he prayed to all that was holy in heaven, on earth, and in hell itself that this would be the last night he would ever spend and the last cussed meal he would ever eat at the wildly renowned establishment in the woods known as Molly B's Inn. Suffering from lack of sleep, a sore back from too soft a mattress, and a stomach ache from a mountain of burnt beans and leather tough eggs, Bill rode out feeling like death warmed over as the growing light of the dawn slowly scrubbed the stars from the sky.

As Bill rode back to the Little Platte, the sky in the east lit up ablaze with yellow, orange, and red streamers of light shooting out from the giant orb of the sun as it dragged itself over the lip of the distant horizon. In its full glory, the sunlight crackled with energy, lighting up every bush and tree. Bill could feel the energy around him and the energy that grew from within his own chest. By the time he arrived at the flat stone along the Little Platte where he and Lucy had agreed to meet, his body seemed to be on the verge of exploding from pent-up anticipation. Dismounting his horse, he found himself in an alien world. Lucy was all he could see in his mind's eye; she was all he could remember about this spot along the river. Nothing else had mattered. Now without the beautiful Lucy and her melodic voice, the only sounds that met his ears were those of babbling waters and a cacophony of bird and insect cries that rose with the morning light. The only sight before his eyes was that of a river and place he had never really seen before.

The banks of the river were low and paved in a carpet of pebbles and rounded stones. The trees and bushes enveloped the river from both sides as it meandered slowly through a tunnel of lush green foliage. Dotting the river banks as though tossed there by mystical fairies were an array of delicate multicolored wildflowers: Dutchman's breeches, blue bells, goat's bread, spider wort, and dogtooth violet, each more wonderous than the next. Beholding the beauty around him only made his desire to see Lucy again even more profound. To calm himself he closed his eyes and breathed deeply, letting the cool floral-scented air wash over him.

After standing motionless for several minutes, Bill walked over and sat down on the flat stone where Lucy had been washing clothes the day before and waited. He strained his ears to listen for any sign of her approach. After nearly an hour he was sure she wouldn't come. Disappointed, he readied himself to leave. Unknown to him, she had been watching him from nearby bushes, torn between her desire to see him again and her fear of where such a meeting may lead. She knew that if she met Bill Barton again, she may not be able to ever forget him or let him go. She also knew that the killer Cole Younger would never let her go. Cole had claimed her for himself, and he would never let her choose another man.

As Bill started to stand up to leave, Lucy could hold herself back no longer. She took a deep breath, and running headlong sprang from the bushes without warning. Surprised, Bill stood up too quickly and found himself balancing precariously just as Lucy reached the flat stone. Her momentum and his unsteady balance sent the two of them headlong into the Little Platte. After making a huge splash, the two struggled to come up for air in the middle of the river.

Startled, standing waist-deep in the river, they looked at each other as they shook their heads and wiped the water out of their eyes. As though on cue, they both began to laugh uncontrollably. For what seemed like an eternity their hysterical laughter echoed off the river banks, up and down the Little Platte. Bill, as though he had known Lucy all his life, took her into his arms and held her tightly. She returned his embrace as they both grew quiet, their breathing nearly silent. Beyond the natural sounds of the babbling waters and the birds and insects around them, they both felt and heard the birth of a new sound, the rhythmic sound of two hearts beating as one.

Once again as though on cue, they both eased their embrace and looked deeply into each other's eyes; each finding the other half of themselves and knowing there could be no other. They then kissed as only lovers kiss, never wanting to let go.

Suddenly coming to her senses, Lucy pushed back on Bill's shoulders and looked him square in the eye. "Bill Barton, you evil demon, get your grubby hands off me," she cried as she pushed and pulled herself away from his embrace.

"What, I, I'm sorry," Bill said, stepping back, flustered by the sudden turn of events.

"You are a demon straight from hell, Bill Barton," Lucy said crossly. "You come around here with your flashing blue eyes and your wily white-toothed smile thinkin' you can sweep any young backcountry bumpkin off her feet."

"I had no intention," Bill said, surprised by the outburst. "And by the way, it was you who swept me off my feet, wasn't it?" Bill continued with a chuckle as he quickly took her hand in his and pulled her to him again. He kissed her deeply and though she pretended to resist at first, she kissed him back, holding him tightly until once again her whole attitude shifted like a swirling leaf caught up in a whirlwind that flips first one way and then the other.

"Damn it, Bill Barton, you are a sneaky lowdown varmint and the devil his self," she barked as she broke free of his embrace. "I'm Cole Younger's woman," Lucy screeched with one hand on her hip and the other hand held up to his face her index finger wagging at him as she spoke. "He said he loves me. He's taken me for his own. He said I was his woman and that he'll kill any man who dares to even touch me," she continued with confidence until she broke down and started to sob, her shoulders jerking up and down uncontrollably.

Bill stepped close to her and once again embraced her tightly. "No one owns you, Lucy, not Cole Younger, not me, not anyone," Bill said, feeling her body shudder as she continued to sob. "What I do know is that we are meant to be together. I felt it the first time I saw you and I know you feel the same about me," Bill continued, his emotions raw as tears streamed from his eyes for the first time in many years.

Lucy looked up at him and resisted at first until their tear-filled eyes met and they both knew the truth. She then melted into his arms as they kissed with abandon, losing themselves in each other. Holding hands, they waded out of the river to a grassy cove that had been cut into the river bank hidden from the main road. Standing in their private world, they once again embraced, losing themselves in each other's arms. As their wet clothing came off, their longing for each other grew more and more urgent. Despite his nearly uncontrollable desire, Bill's movements remained slow and gentle. Lucy had never experienced such tenderness in a man. Cole had always been rough and quick to satisfy himself with little regard to her feelings or desires. With Bill, she felt as if they moved as one, and as their passions fulfilled rose together, she understood for the first time in her life what making love really meant.

In their innocence, they laid in each other's arms naked and unashamed, their hearts beating as one. Bill and Lucy felt as though they were the only humans on Earth as they held each other tight and looked in wonder at the lush green paradise that surrounded them. Moved deeply by the experience, Bill wondered aloud whether Adam and Eve had shared similar experiences of ecstasy in the Garden of Eden long ago. Looking deeply into each other's eyes, they both knew they felt the same way. Their union, though consummated by the natural yearning of two young bodies for each other, was one that transcended mere pleasures of the flesh. They also knew they would soon be banished from their blissful Eden and pursued relentlessly to the ends of the Earth by the devil himself, the cold-blooded killer, Cole Younger.

After getting dressed into clothing still damp from their dip in the Little Platte, they spent the next few hours talking and getting to know each other. Their fears, hopes, and dreams were all shared. By late morning they began making plans for their future. Bill would ride on to Westport and then to Kansas City to look for possible options for their escape. Lucy would get her things ready to travel with Bill. All would need to be done in secret as they both knew that Cole Younger was not the kind of killer anyone would want to meet head on. They would need to make a run for it and hope Cole never found out which way they went.

After a long sweet good-bye, Bill finally rode out of Buchanan County and headed for Westport. He crossed the Missouri River by ferry at Independence. His mind raced as he mulled over the loose plan he and Lucy had cooked up. Bill had been careful not to let Lucy know what business he needed to take care of in Kansas City. He had told her that after he completed his business, he would withdraw all the money he had saved up in a bank in Kansas City. With the money in hand, they would be able to make a run for it the first chance they got. Where they would go and how they would get out of Missouri alive presented them with plenty of unknowns. They were determined, however, to find a way. Their biggest obstacle would be eluding the grip of Cole Younger and his brothers. Not knowing when and where Cole might pop up next made things even tougher.

Bill knew the Youngers lived near Lee Summit in Jackson County, not far south of Westport and Kansas City. Despite being well-known outlaws, the Younger boys, Cole, Jim, Bob, and John, never failed to come back to their family farm and to their loving mother, Bursheba. The local law in Jackson County chose to look the other way rather than face down the Younger Gang. Fact was, folks in the area backed the South during the war and would back the Youngers to the death, if it came to that. Other rural folk around the area either supported the Youngers' resistance to the occupation of the South after the war by federal troops or idealized their notorious exploits. The rest simply feared what would happen to themselves and their loved ones if they ever spoke out against the Youngers.

Bill knew if their plans failed to pan out, or if things ever went haywire, they wouldn't be able to rely on local folk anywhere in the state of Missouri for aid or comfort. The plain fact was, southern sympathizers outnumbered Union supporters two to one in many parts of the state. Bill had to maintain his cover as Leroy Thompson and get things done right the first time. From here on, as he thought about Molly B's many suspicions and her possible connection to Cole Younger, he would need to be on the lookout for any prying eyes. One slip could be his last.

Bill never shared the fact with anyone that he had been a Union spy during the war. When asked what he did during the war, his cover story had always been that he fought as a Union Army regular. Cole Younger, on the other hand, had been a Confederate guerilla fighter. Cole and Bill had never come face to face with one another. Bill was certain Cole wouldn't know him if the two men ever happened to bump into one another or pass each other on an empty street. Bill's advantage was that he could identify Cole Younger on sight, having seen him up close more than once during his years working undercover in the South.

In a queer twist of fate, Bill had run into Jesse and Frank James one moonless night when they found themselves rustling the same cattle. Rather than shooting it out, Bill, using his alias Leroy Thompson, had amicably agreed to split the cattle with the James brothers. As was the case with so many poor rural farm folks after the war, the James brothers had come home to tough times. They had seen no problem with working together with Leroy Thompson, a fellow southerner, to rustle a few head of cattle to make ends meet.

While Bill stuck with rustling cattle, the James brothers turned to gunplay and highway robbery, eventually teaming up with the Younger brothers and becoming the notorious James-Younger Gang. Beyond robbing stagecoaches, banks, and trains simply for the cash and gold, Jesse James claimed the robberies were part of his larger agenda of revenge and vendetta against corrupt Yankees and Reconstruction carpetbaggers. Though Jesse claimed he did what he did for a righteous cause, Bill knew there was more than a little truth in what Frank James had shared with him about Jesse. After living for years on the run as a guerilla fighter, Jesse had simply grown too fond of the outlaw life to ever give it up. Jesse sought fame and notoriety for himself more than any righteous cause; Bill, on the other hand, like most cattle rustlers and horse thieves, sought only anonymity under the cover of darkness and a faceless mask.

Though he stayed in the shadows, Bill Barton was no bargain when it came to gun play. He was more than a fair shot and was quick on the draw. He had drawn blood and taken down more than a few men since taking up his outlaw ways. Post-war Missouri was a lawless land full of bushwhackers and rogues. Bill had shot his way out of plenty of close scrapes. As he left a blood-stained trail behind him, Leroy Thompson's reputation had become widely known in outlaw circles. He wasn't a man to be tested. The line Bill wouldn't cross was robbing innocent folks or killing in cold blood. Anyone who had caught Bill's lead had been throwing his own first. Bill wasn't cut out to be an outlaw; he was a soldier. His only mission had been to build back his fortune by stealing from the southern scum who had taken everything from him and his family. Though this was the story he liked to tell himself, he had to admit, like Jesse, he too had grown fond of the outlaw life. He also knew the longer he ran with desperadoes, the greater his chances of spending the rest of his life on the run.

When he heard that the James and Younger brothers had joined forces, it had come as no surprise to Bill. Cole Younger and Frank James had both ridden with William Quantrill himself and Jesse James with "Bloody-Bill" Anderson. They shared a battle-hardened bond as many warriors do who have fought and bled together. Once Jesse and Cole took to the ways of gunslinging outlaws, Bill gave them a wide berth, avoiding ever having their paths cross.

Bill was counting on the fact that though the James brothers might remember Leroy Thompson and what he looked like, Leroy was a total stranger to Cole Younger and his brothers; that was an ace in the hole he would need to play should they ever come face to face.

May 3, 1867

Little Platte River, Buchanan County, Missouri

Perilous Future

AFTER BILL RODE OUT for Westport, Lucy sat on the flat stone beside the running waters of the Little Platte for a long time thinking about how her life had been forever changed. She loved Bill Barton with all her body and soul. Though their escape from the grip of Cole Younger and his brothers wouldn't be easy, she prayed they would find a way. She knew Cole was growing impatient. She knew he wanted to marry her. She shivered as she thought of Cole forcing himself on her again and feared he would soon take her from her home and from Pappy forever. No one wanted to stand up to the Youngers. They were above the law in these parts. Whatever a Younger wanted, he took, and no one challenged his right to do so. She feared her situation was hopeless and that she had now put Bill in mortal danger.

Bill loved her, she knew this with all her heart. She believed him when he told her that he would never let her go. It was this truth that troubled her most. Lucy feared Cole would kill Bill if he ever found out Bill planned to take her from him. As her mind whirled, seeking possible ways to escape Cole's clutches, a barking growl came from the trail above.

"Lucy, you down there?" Molly B hollered as she pushed her way through the brush lining the river bank.

"Molly B, that you?" Lucy shouted back as she got to her feet.

"Well hell girl, you are a sight. What ya been doin'? You been taking a bath with all your clothes on?" Molly B said, seeing Lucy standing on a flat stone next to the river, her hair and clothing still visibly damp.

"Oh, no, I thought I saw something shiny in the water and slipped when I reached for it. Next thing I knew I was laying in the middle of the river. Damnedest thing. I'm just sitting here trying to dry off," Lucy lied, pretending to laugh at her own folly.

"Oh, that sounds like a hell of thing. Well at least you don't seem any worse for wear," Molly B said looking her over like a butcher might size up a side of beef. "What were you doing down here so early?" she continued as she tilted her head to one side, her unblinking cockeye probing Lucy's every reaction.

"I thought I forgot some laundry here yesterday evening and came back to search for it this mornin'," Lucy lied, her mind racing to respond to the unexpected inquisition.

"So, you were here yesterday evening and came back this morning. Find anything?" Molly B said, nodding her massive head. "See anybody?" she continued, her cockeye searching for the truth.

"No, no, on both counts," Lucy said a bit too quickly. She could feel her cheeks flush as she tried desperately to appear calm. She wondered why Molly B had come down to the river at this early hour, something she had never done in the past.

"Too bad you lost that laundry. A gal wouldn't want to go around without her bloomers pulled up tight," Molly B said, looking around, and suddenly surprised to find Lucy's bloomers hanging out to dry on a nearby bush. "Are you sure you didn't run into a handsome rider yesterday evening or maybe this mornin'? I had a payin' guest last night. He rode in yesterday evening and rode out south this mornin'. I thought he might've come this way," she continued, her cockeye ever vigilant.

"I'm sure the laundry will turn up. Probably in the woods between here and Pappy's cabin. As for riders, I haven't seen any, yesterday or this mornin'," Lucy said flatly, her hands on her hips.

Molly B noticed fresh horseshoe tracks nearby but decided not to push the topic any further. She was pretty sure the horseshoe tracks with their distinctive V-mark at the tips belonged to Leroy Thompson since they matched perfectly with the ones his horse had left at her place. She was also sure Lucy was lying. She wondered what might have happened between Leroy and Lucy. She suspected it was nothing Cole Younger would look kindly on. Lucy's bloomers hanging out to dry by the river with fresh tracks nearby was more than a little disturbing.

Since Cole had taken up courting Lucy, no other man had dared to even approach her. This had made Molly B's job easy. Leroy Thompson, however, was no local bumpkin. She had watched him cleaning his guns the night before and saw how he handled them like a professional. The risk of a run-in with Cole Younger might not be enough to spook off the likes of Leroy Thompson. She feared Leroy already had ideas of his own. Molly B reasoned she would need to keep a much closer eye on Lucy and a sharp lookout for Leroy Thompson.

She knew Leroy had said he was going to Westport to look for work on a wagon train. If true, he wouldn't be back anytime soon. Molly B decided however to take no chances. Cole paid her well. If she wanted to collect what he owed her, she would need to make sure Lucy stayed put and remained Cole's woman.

Lucy and Molly B finally said their farewells and went off in opposite directions. Lucy noticed Molly B hadn't been carrying a gun for hunting, a pole for fishing, or laundry for washing. Lucy knew there were no other good reasons for Molly B to be out along the Little Platte River at this hour of the morning. Considering how Molly B had acted, Lucy recalled Pappy's warning that Cole Younger might have hired spies to watch her now that he had set his sights on having her for himself. Lucy headed back home, certain Molly B was one of those spies paid by Cole Younger to keep an eye on her. The thought of Molly B spying on her sent a chill down her spine since she had unwittingly sent Bill straight to Molly B's Inn the evening before. Because of this, Molly B now knew what Bill looked like and would be on the lookout for him. Lucy knew Bill would be coming back in a few days, unaware he might be watched or even bushwhacked. She felt helpless with no way to warn Bill of the menace Molly B posed.

With all that could go wrong and with Molly B lurking about, she wondered whether they would be able to keep their plans secret until they made a run for it. She also had no idea when Cole would pop up again. His biggest threat had always been his unpredictability. He tended to come and go without warning. What worried her most was that killing came easy for Cole and his brothers. As she made her trek home, her concern for Bill grew with every step as she thought about the unknown and perilous future they both now faced.

May 3, 1867

Agency, Buchanan County, Missouri

Real Belle of the Ball

MOLLY B WATCHED AS Lucy disappeared into the woods leading to Pappy's cabin. She couldn't shake her suspicion that something had happened between Leroy Thompson and Lucy Breeden right here along the Little Platte. How Leroy had acted the night before and the way he had answered her questions about seeing anyone along the river had made her suspect he might have met Lucy and was for some reason trying to hide the fact. And now this morning to find Lucy by the river without any obvious chores to do and with her clothing wet and her bloomers hanging out to dry only added to the mystery. Molly B knew Cole's heart was set on making Lucy his woman. He had warned Molly B that if he couldn't have Lucy, no one would. Molly B knew what he meant and that he meant it.

Molly B had learned about Cole's quick and violent temper the hard way. She recalled Cole's reaction to rumors she had shared about his love affair with Myra Maybelle Shirley from Carthage, Missouri, and that many believed she was still his sweetheart. Molly B had no more than gotten the words out of her mouth when Cole blew his top. She rubbed her lip as she recalled how his denial of the rumors had been intense and violent.

"God damn it, Molly B, I've never had no designs on Belle Shirley. Now, who's the son-of-a-bitch who says I have?" Cole barked as he slapped Molly B hard across her mouth with the back of his hand. The blow, taking her by surprise, nearly knocked her off her feet.

"I heard the rumors in town. Just some ignorant country folk goin' on about other people's business, that's all it was, Cole," Molly B said as even-tempered as she could, her own temper nearing the boiling point as her split lip oozed a thick stream of blood down her chin.

"You ever bring it up again and I'll drive my fist right through that ugly face of yours, comprende?" Cole growled as he glared at Molly B, with his right fist clenched in a hard ball.

In reply, Molly B could only hold her hands up, palms out in front of her. She feared if she uttered another word, Cole wouldn't be able to hold himself in check. She knew she could take Cole in a fair fight. If she ever got ahold of him, she could rip the man in half and they both knew it. She also knew if she tried, he could pull his pistol faster than greased lighting and empty it into her, point-blank, before she ever laid a hand on him.

Molly B had to admit, the facts seemed to be on Cole's side. Belle, as Myra Maybelle liked to be called, had married her teenage sweetheart Jim Reed not more than a year ago in 1866. There was no way Cole would be courting a married woman, especially a woman married to Jim Reed, widely known to be one of Cole's best friends.

Cole and Jim Younger had known Jim Reed since childhood. Like the James brothers and Cole and Jim Younger, Jim Reed and Bud Shirley, Belle's brother, had ridden with Quantrill's Raiders. Their bonds were deep and none of them would do anything to harm the other. Belle's father, Judge Shirley, had been a Confederate sympathizer. After being burnt out of their home in Carthage in Jasper County, Missouri, the Shirley family had moved to Scyene, Texas, near Dallas. The judge supported the Confederate cause throughout the war even after Bud, his only son, was killed in an ambush in 1864.

After the war, the judge continued to hide and give aid and comfort to former Quantrill Raiders who had turned outlaw. The Younger brothers, James brothers, Jim Reed, and others had often taken refuge at the Shirley place in Texas. Everyone knew Belle. They also knew she had been sweet on Jim Reed, her childhood sweetheart in Carthage. Cole and the other men who came and went became part of Belle's extended family, more a merry band of brothers than probable sweethearts. Belle being a wild one, however, led Molly B to suspect Jim Reed hadn't been Belle's only lover and that Cole Younger may very well have been one of them.

Molly B thought it strange Cole never talked about having a woman and no one seemed to ever mention Cole having a lover or even a sweetheart. The only rumor she had ever heard was that Cole had strong feelings for Belle Shirley. Molly B had no idea whether Cole had ever had eyes for

Belle. What she did know was how Cole looked at Lucy Breeden and how it seemed damn clear that Lucy meant a great deal to him. Beyond his desire to have Lucy and to keep her for his own, Cole truly seemed to be in love with the little half-breed, or at least in love with the thought of having her many pleasures for himself. In Molly B's scheming mind, she had no doubts about how Cole felt about Lucy. She also had no doubts about how Lucy Breeden felt about Cole. What was clear to anyone who cared to look was that Lucy felt no love for Cole Younger, only fear.

Soon after Cole met Lucy near the Little Platte for the first time, he had asked Pappy, Lucy's father, for permission to court his daughter. Pappy, upon learning who Cole Younger was, had agreed without objection. Molly B knew Pappy had little choice but to accept Cole's request considering what his refusal would have meant for him and Lucy. Cole was used to getting what he wanted. If he didn't get it when he demanded it, he simply took it, often by violence. Soon after Cole started courting the lovely Lucy Breeden, he had asked Molly B to keep a close eye on her. Cole wanted no one to come near Lucy and if anyone did, Cole wanted to be the first to know.

The deal Cole and Molly B struck was that Molly B would report to Cole by telegram twice a month. To do this, the arrangement was for Molly B to ride to the nearby small town of Agency in Buchanan County and to send Cole a telegram update every other week. If Cole had special instructions for Molly B, he would let her know by telegram as well. His messages would be waiting for Molly B to pick up when she came to Agency to send her bi-weekly report. Molly B knew she needed to get to Agency as soon as possible. It was time for her to make her report and to see if Cole had sent any special instructions for her. She would need to share her suspicions about Leroy Thompson and knew this would upset Cole. Even so, if she failed to report her suspicions and something happened, it might be the last thing she failed to do above ground.

For Molly B, Lucy was her golden goose. There was no way she would let the little Indian princess stop laying golden eggs. At two hundred dollars a month, the fee Cole was paying for her services, Molly B only hoped the courtship of Lucy Breeden would continue smoothly well into the future. The thought of a long courtship brought a grizzly gap-toothed smile across her greasy whiskered face. Her small narrow-set eyes lit up with the vision of gold coins paving the trail in front of her all the way to the horizon and she imagined all the way north to Alaska as she spurred her swaybacked steed into a fast trot. She figured she would make Agency by noon and have plenty of time after she took care of business to get back home long before nightfall. For Molly B, the future looked mighty bright with her grubstake growing fatter by the month.

May 3, 1867

Kingston, Caldwell County, Missouri

The Odd Dollar

"OPEN THE VAULT YOU jittery-fingered bastard!" Jesse barked, causing the bank teller's hands to tremble and twitch even harder as he struggled to work the combination lock.

"Everyone else, listen up," Cole growled from the other side of the room getting everyone's attention. "If you want to live, don't move and stay quiet," he added as he held two six-shooters on a group of hostages made up of bank staff and customers who had been herded into a back corner of the bank lobby.

Cole became concerned that their time in the bank seemed to be stretching on without end. Tension was growing by the minute. He knew if things went on much longer, Jesse's hair-trigger temper might blow. If it did, Jesse could start plugging holes in the bank teller and more than a few of the hostages. Cole knew if things went sideways, he might have to throw a little lead himself. Killing to drive home a point was justified in Cole Younger's world. During his years of hit-and-run guerrilla warfare with William Quantrill, he had killed plenty of men in cold blood to make a point or to simply even a score. Jesse had told him that after Bloody-Bill Anderson was gunned down in a Union Army ambush near Albany, Missouri in October 1864, they found a rope on his body with 54 knots tied in it. Cole wondered how many knots would be tied in his rope had he kept track. He suspected it might be a damn sight more than 54 by now.

"God damn it, I said hurry up!" Jesse growled, striking the teller on the forehead with the butt of his pistol, opening a deep gash which began to bleed profusely. The teller wobbled from the blow, staggered forward, his legs buckling, leaving him on his knees in front of Jesse.

"Please, mister, I'm tryin' my best," the teller pleaded, holding up both hands in a hapless attempt to forestall any further blows.

"Your best ain't been good enough," Jesse hissed. "Now get ahold of yourself, you little bastard, and open this goddamn vault and I mean pronto, or I will blow your goddamn brains out. Right here, right now!" Jesse barked with such force and conviction in the tone of voice that no one within ear shot doubted for a second that he would do exactly what he said.

The teller redoubled his efforts as blood streamed down his face, soaking his shirt and dripping onto the polished marble floor. When the door of the vault finally swung open, Jesse singled out two women from the hostages and motioned for them to enter the vault and quickly fill the bags he threw to them with as much cash and gold coin as possible. Watched closely, the women scooped up stacks of cash and handfuls of gold coins, filling the two bags until they could hold no more.

Grabbing the bags and waving the ladies and the bloodied teller back to join the rest of the hostages, Jesse and Cole slowly backed their way out of the bank while holding their guns on the frightened group huddled in the corner. Closing the door behind them, Cole and Jesse exchanged a quick glance and breathed a sigh of relief; they had pulled off the robbery without firing a single shot. They were doubly relieved knowing the folks in the surrounding area had supported the Confederacy and Quantrill's Raiders during the war. Killing a few blue-bellied devils was one thing, killing former comrades was quite another.

In front of the bank, Bob, John, and Jim Younger guarded the street from both directions while Frank James and Charlie Pitts waited with guns drawn and holding the reins of Jesse's and Cole's horses. When Jesse and Cole hit the street, Frank and Charlie tossed each man the reins to his horse. They quickly mounted. With every man in his saddle, the seven men slapped leather to the flanks of their horses, spurring them into a gallop and leaving the town of Kingston behind them in a cloud of dust.

The men rode straight east and then one way and then another until they were sure they had covered their trail and were in the clear. If there was a posse, it would have a tough time finding their tracks or even figuring out which way they rode.

During their long ride the men rode in silence, focused only on covering their tracks and putting distance between themselves and their last bank robbery.

The long silent ride drove each man deep into his own thoughts. Cole couldn't help thinking of the beautiful Lucy Breeden. He had long since made up his mind that he would marry her first chance he got. Courting her had been tough. She had politely resisted his affections at every turn for months. She had finally yielded to him during their last encounter. He grinned at the thought of how she had fought like a cornered she-lion against his embrace until she had yielded to him for the first time. Like breaking any wild mustang, she put up one hell of a fight until she gave him full rein. He believed with all his heart that in that moment, she had become his woman. She was his Lucy-belle and he would kill any man who dared to take her from him. In the end, he reasoned, she was no different than any other woman. She had needed a man's firm hand to guide her to her place in the world. She now belonged to him.

According to ol' Molly B, Lucy hadn't had any gentlemen callers since Cole had taken an interest. Once the local boys knew who was courting Lucy Breeden, they soon gave her a wide berth. Cole paid Molly B well to keep an eye on Lucy, even if it was a cockeye, Cole thought as he chuckled to himself. He knew his Lucy-belle was his and that she would grow closer to him in time. Though he was confident Lucy-belle was his woman, Cole was a prideful jealous man and worried she might be stolen away from him by another man in his absence.

The sudden shock and pain of losing his first true love still sat heavy on his heart. Judge John Shirley from Carthage, Missouri had always actively supported the Confederate cause, providing aid and comfort to Quantrill's guerrilla fighters. Myra Maybelle, known as Belle, was the judge's beautiful daughter who caught the eye of every man she ever met. For Cole, it was love at first sight. Though Cole had never shared his feelings for Belle Shirley with anyone, Cole and Belle had become lovers during the war. Their secret relationship continued after the war, though Cole was unable to see her as often as he would have liked. In his heart, Belle was the love of his life, until unexpectedly not more than a year ago she up and married Jim Reed, a fellow Quantrill Raider and one of Cole's best friends.

Upon hearing the good tidings, Cole swore a blood oath to himself that he would never lose another woman to any man, friend or foe. Lucy-belle would be his and his alone. He would kill anyone who tried to take her from him. Cole had already sent a message to inform Molly B he would be coming for Lucy no later than May 5. He figured Molly B would get his message when she sent him her regular report. Though he wouldn't have any way to receive Molly B's report on Lucy before heading out to Buchanan County, he no longer felt it made any difference. He smiled to himself at the thought of soon enjoying the many delicious delights of Lucy-belle Breeden every night for the rest of his life. The only thing he needed now to tie the knot was a respectable wedding ring.

After their long ride, the gang reached an old lean-to, not ten miles from Kingston, that they had used in the past. The men quickly dismounted and led their horses out of view from the road. Jesse was already counting money when the others stepped into the lean-to.

"We need to do this quick. Cole, you count that other bag. It looks like we got over ten thousand dollars here," Jesse said without looking up as he continued to count, splitting the money into five-hundred-dollar stacks.

Most of the money was paper with a few silver coins thrown in. About a third of the loot was in gold coins. Jesse and Cole worked for several minutes, counting and making rows of neatly stacked bills and coins.

"Cole, what's your count? I have 5,633 dollars in cash and dollar coins and 2,350 dollars in gold coins," Jesse said leaning back on the log stool he was sitting on.

"I have 3,454 dollars in cash and silver and 1,500 dollars in gold," Cole announced.

"That's 9,087 dollars in cash and silver and 3,850 dollars in gold. For a grand total of 12,937 dollars," Charlie Pitts said matter-of-factly. "Divided seven ways that's 1,298 dollars in cash and silver coins and 550 dollars in gold each. A total of 1,848 dollars for each man. A pretty good day's wages I'd say. We'll let Jesse and Cole flip that last silver dollar to settle on the big winner. Wouldn't want anyone fighting over it," he concluded with a wink, setting off a ripple of laughter that filled the little lean-to.

Every man there knew Charlie Pitts was dead right on his count of the money. If Charlie said that was how much everyone would get in a seven-way split, everyone there was sure that is exactly how it would work out. How Charlie did his calculations so fast, no one ever ventured to ask.

Once the money was divided, the men discovered what they all already knew, Charlie's math was correct, right down to the last odd dollar. Once each man had his share of the loot, he quickly left the lean-to, mounted his horse, and rode out. From here on, each man would ride alone, steering his own course home.

"Jesse, you can keep the last odd dollar, I'll keep the next one," Cole said as he flipped a silver dollar to Jesse.

Jesse plucked the shiny silver Morgan dollar out of the air and swiftly tucked the coin into his shirt pocket, buttoning the flap in a single move. "See you soon. Don't do anything I wouldn't do in Kansas City. That place can be the downfall of any man," Jesse said with a wink and a nod as he spurred his horse and was gone. He knew they would come together again in a few months when things settled down.

Charlie Pitts and Cole Younger were the last two riders to hit the trail. The others had already ridden out in separate directions, each man with his own destination in mind. Cole tipped his hat to Charlie and headed straight for Kansas City. With over 6,000 dollars in his saddlebags, his brothers having loaned him 1,500 dollars each from their shares of the loot, Cole figured he now had enough cash to buy the best damn wedding ring Kansas City had to offer. Charlie Pitts, with only gambling and whores on his mind, headed straight for the card tables in Westport.

May 3, 1867

Westport, Jackson County, Missouri

Value of an Ace

CHARLIE PITTS RODE INTO Westport early evening and couldn't wait to find a friendly game of Black Jack. Charlie with his uncanny math skills found that he was a natural-born card counter. If he could just get into a game for a few hours, he knew he might even double the money he had in his saddlebags. If anyone caught on to his little tricks, he knew he might have to throw a little hot lead around and head for the hills. He chuckled to himself at the thought of running off with big wads of cash stuffed in his saddlebags and his guns blazing, cutting down everything and everyone in his path.

Saloons, dance halls, whorehouses, and gambling parlors lined the streets of Westport's entertainment district. Piano music rang from every doorway as the sounds of laughter and merriment filled the air. The smell of horse shit, stale cigar smoke, sour sweat, and sweet toilette water permeated every nook and cranny of the place. Charlie inhaled deeply and surveyed the scene unfolding around him as he slowly rode down the middle of the street, loving every scent and sight.

"Hey cowboy, ya lookin' fer some company?" yelled a large bosomed blond, one leg propped up on a boardwalk bench as she worked the strap on her garter, revealing more than a little of the merchandise. Charlie liked what he saw, but knew she wasn't the only soiled dove he would run into tonight. Having always liked big-breasted blonds, he thought he might even come back to look this one up. Charlie tipped his hat, gave her a quick smile and a wink, and rode on up the street.

Charlie hadn't gone very far when a short barrel-chested man with a gimpy right leg came bounding into the street waving both arms. "Charlie, you ol' son-of-a-gun, it's me, Billy. What the hell you doin' in Westport?" As he spoke, Billy Chadwell took hold of the bridle of Charlie's horse. Billy and Charlie went way back. Billy had ridden with the James-Younger Gang on a couple jobs when the gang first came together. Charlie hadn't seen Billy in a coon's age.

"Billy you ol' cuss. Where you been holed up? Haven't seen hide nor hair of ya for near on a year now," Charlie said as he slid down off his horse to meet Billy eye to eye. The two men clapped each other on the shoulder and shook hands.

"You headed anywhere special?" Billy asked.

"No, just lookin' for a good Black Jack game if'n I can find one," Charlie said, looking at the saloons on both sides of the street.

"I know just the place, the Big Badger Saloon, just up the way. They have more tables dealing Black Jack than any other place on the street," Billy said, pointing the way.

"First things first, how about a drink or three for ol' times sake? I'd like to hear about what might be cookin', if'n you catch me drift," Billy added in a low voice. "Damn Pinkerton spies are everywhere, best to take our jabbering inside," Billy continued, giving a quick look over his shoulder.

Charlie guided his horse in front of the Big Badger and tied his reins to a hitching post with a watering trough. The ride into Westport had been a dry and dusty one and he knew his horse had to be just as thirsty as he was. Grabbing his saddlebags, he joined Billy. The two men waltzed into the saloon together, one doing the two-step and the other hobbling to keep up.

Billy and Charlie sat in the back corner of the saloon where they could keep an eye on all the comings and goings. After Charlie threw two twenty-dollar gold pieces on the table, he told the barmaid to keep the drinks coming, but to leave the two of them alone. After the barmaid brought back a bottle of the saloon's best whisky, she poured each man a drink and left the bottle on the table. Charlie waited to speak until she hustled out of earshot.

"Toast, my good man. May fortune shine on you once again in the not-too-distant future," Charlie said with a wink and a nod. The two men clinked their glasses together and downed their drinks in a single gulp.

"Now tell me, Charlie, how can a few piles of those little shiny gold critters find their way in to ol' Billy's pockets sooner rather than later?" Billy motioned toward the two twenty-dollar gold pieces.

"Well to be honest, Billy, your gimpy leg is a real drawback for the kind of jobs we been pullin' lately, especially train jobs. If we pull another bank job where we need a dependable gun hand, we'd sure like to have you ridin' with us again. You're a hell of a quick draw and a dead aim with a six-shooter from the back of a horse. With all the lead flyin' around lately, we might need more men who can shoot and shoot straight," Charlie said, not sure how much he should be sharing with Billy just yet.

"You can always count on me, Charlie. You got killin' to do, I'm not afraid to pull the trigger," Billy said with a growl in his voice that left Charlie with no doubt he could still count on Billy if he had to.

"Always best to get in and out without firin' a shot. Tends to give a man a better chance of livin' long enough to spend all the loot," Charlie said as the two men laughed at the thought of having time on their hands and a pile of loot to spend.

Charlie and Billy drank their first bottle of whiskey and ordered another before they had a couple of large T-bone steaks for supper. Billy had been living near Westport on a small farm for the past year. Charlie now knew where Billy lived and how to contact him when the time came. He promised to contact him should Jesse ask for additional gun hands in the future. He also told ol' Billy that Jesse had been working on finding out where the carpetbaggers were stowing all their loot up north. The whole gang hoped Jesse would figure it out before too long. A job that big would be a bonanza, a pile of loot so huge that it would set everyone up for life. Charlie added that a robbery like that would teach those Yankee bastards a lesson, though in his heart he couldn't care less. He had added the comment out of habit in deference to Jesse. Jesse viewed the robbery as part of his grand crusade against northern oppression. For the most part, the rest of the James-Younger Gang just wanted to get rich before they got killed.

Soon after arriving in Westport, Bill had met with Mr. Theodor Jeffers in front of Delmonico's Diner on Main Street. Mr. Jeffers, a cattle buyer from St. Louis, had been honest with Bill when he told him why he had requested a first meeting in Westport. He simply wanted to see the town where both the Santa Fe and Oregon Trails began. Jeffers was excited by tales of Wild West adventure, though he himself as a native of Boston had never ventured further west than St. Louis. Jeffers was delighted to have Bill show him around.

During a quick walking tour of the town followed by a steak dinner at Delmonico's, Bill played the role of tour guide and host. Theodor was excited about being at the doorstep of the untamed west. He was amazed at how busy the town was with its churn of cowboys, frontier men, Indian scouts, gamblers, merchants, and an endless stream of settlers flowing in from the east still wet behind the ears. Bill pointed out that trade in Westport had fallen off sharply since the war and that Kansas City had taken the lead. With further expansion of the railroads, Westport's boom days were behind it. Before Jeffers returned to Kansas City both men had agreed to meet the next day at the Kansas City stockyard as per earlier communications. Freed of escort duties, Bill decided to have a few drinks and call it a night. Bill spied an empty stool at the bar in the Big Badger Saloon as he walked by and decided it was as good as any.

The stool was a good one in that it provided him with a clear view of the bat-winged doors. After years of living undercover, his spy craft seemed to come as second nature. Having no more than received his first drink from the bartender, Bill nearly spilt the full glass of whiskey down the front of his shirt when he was suddenly startled by the appearance of two men he had never expected to see pushing their way through the saloon's swinging doors. He was sure the man on the right was Charlie Pitts: his long horse face, piggy eyes, bushy eyebrows, and crooked smile were unmistakable. The man on the left was Billy Chadwell. The man's short stature, barrel chest, and noticeable limp—a present he received from the Union Army at Gettysburg he told anyone who cared to ask—made Billy an easy target to pick out in a crowd.

Charlie Pitts and Cole Younger were close friends. Billy and Charlie were also close, having grown up together. Bill knew both men were on-again off-again members of the James-Younger Gang. Just after the war, Bill had ridden with both Billy Chadwell and Charlie Pitts to rustle a few head of cattle and to steal a horse or two. Like Jesse and Frank, Billy and Charlie had no problem teaming up with a fellow southerner to make little quick cash. Since they joined the James-Younger Gang however, Bill had harbored no desire to seek out either man and had actively avoided ever running into them. Now here they both were as big as life. Bill wondered how, without raising suspicion, he might learn the whereabouts of Cole Younger from one of the two men. Bill decided to bide his time and sip his whiskey. He would wait until the men split up to see which one he might be able to safely approach.

After polishing off a bottle and a half of whiskey and two huge bloody steaks, Billy and Charlie said their farewells. Billy was clearly drunk as he wobbled and hobbled his way through the saloon's bat-winged doors and back out onto the boardwalk.

As soon as Billy parted, Charlie made a beeline straight to the card tables in the back of the saloon.

❧

Though he was a little tipsy, Charlie's mind was still crystal clear. If nothing else, Charlie Pitts was a man who could hold his liquor. Spying the Black Jack tables, it took Charlie no time to cross the room and slide into an empty seat. "Give me chips and deal me in," he said, slamming down a five-hundred-dollar stack of gold coins on the table.

The dealer scooped up the coins, checked the amount and handed Charlie five hundred dollars in chips. The other players at the table waited for the transaction until the dealer barked, "Place your bets!" To Charlie, he added with a smirk, "five-dollar minimum, buckaroo."

Charlie put down a five-dollar chip and started counting cards. He would bet low for the first twenty hands or so; by then he would have the measure of things and would be ready to bet some serious money.

Five players sat at the table and the dealer was dealing from a six-deck stack. Charlie had to laugh at the futile attempt by the casino to frustrate card counters. Fact was, more decks increased the accuracy of a card counter like Charlie. He knew this would be a good night when by the eighteenth hand his predictions of cards for every player were nearly spot-on.

When Charlie suddenly started betting fifty and a hundred dollars a hand and winning nearly every time, the dealer started watching him closely. Charlie noticed when the dealer motioned to the pit boss to pay Charlie more attention. Charlie knew that after a few more hands he would be asked to leave. Politely at first and not so politely if he refused. He had already won over two thousand dollars and knew his time was growing short.

Just as the pit boss and two other malicious-looking gentlemen started to move in on the table, Charlie quickly stood up and dragged his chips into his hat.

"Well boys, looks like tonight was my lucky night. Thought I better quit while I'm still ahead for a change," Charlie said, throwing his saddlebags over his shoulder and hugging his chip-filled hat to his chest. "If'n you'd be so kind as to point me to the cashier, I'll be on my way," Charlie said, looking into the grim face of the dealer, who pointed to a cashier's cage at the far end of the room.

Before stepping away from the table, Charlie flipped a five-dollar chip at the dealer, hitting him square in the face. "That buckaroo is your tip, my five-dollar minimum," Charlie said with a taunting chuckle. The dealer, unable to leave his station, stood red-faced and fuming as he glared at Charlie who wasted no time in hustling off toward the cashier's cage.

The pit boss and his lackies soon flanked Charlie in midstride. Attempting to avoid a public scene, they hemmed Charlie in while the pit boss delivered his warning through tight thin lips into Charlie's left ear. "We don't take kindly to card counters in Westport. I suggest you be on your way out of town or you can count on us paying you a less-than-friendly social call this evening." The viper-like hissing sound of the pit boss's voice made Charlie recoil. He would need to watch his back until he was clear of Westport if he wanted to stay alive long enough to spend his hard-earned cash. He would soon have nearly four thousand dollars in his saddlebags, more than double what he came in with, and more than enough to get any man killed.

After safely cashing out, Charlie headed for safer environs. As he rode back up the street, the buxom blond was still flashing her wares. Charlie motioned for her to follow him. He had seen a grand-looking hotel on Main Street that he was sure had a safe where guests could leave their valuables for the night. If he could get things tucked away tight and proper, there would be no harm in sampling the lady's wares, he thought, as a wicked crooked smile spread across his narrow pock-ridden face, making him look more like a deranged madman on a mission from hell than a man out for a little evening entertainment.

Seeing that Charlie had his heart set on playing cards, Bill had caught up with Billy Chadwell on the boardwalk and offered to buy him a drink. Billy was happy to see the ol' horse thief Leroy Thompson again and told him how he had just run into a mutual friend of theirs, ol' Charlie Pitts. The two men soon found themselves at a table in the back of the Red Garter Saloon. Bill plied the already-drunk Billy Chadwell with one whiskey after another in hopes of gathering information about the whereabouts of the James-Younger Gang. After more than a few drinks, Bill became convinced Billy was no longer in the loop. His bum leg had made him of little use to the gang. Just when Bill was ready to call it a night, unexpectedly Billy shared a bit of vital information with him that he would later find to be invaluable.

"Yeah, yeah, ol' Charlie'll be gettin' ahol't of me when they got gun work to do. Everyone knows I can shoot straight and won't hesitate to kill anything movin', if'n I have to," Billy boasted, red-faced as he stared through blood-shot eyes into his half-full whiskey glass. "Charlie says Jesse is plannin' on a big job someplace up north. Says he'll fill me in later when Jesse shares his plan. Says the job will be the big one, the one that'll put anyone who rides with the James-Younger Gang on easy street," Billy babbled, his speech so slurred it was nearly unintelligible.

Finishing his drink, Billy said his farewells, staggered out of the Red Garter, and headed home. Bill was amazed Billy could still stand up, let alone find his horse and get up into his saddle using a stump as a stairstep due to his bum leg. Bill followed Billy at a distance all the way back to his place south of Westport. Bill was sure the Pinkertons might find it interesting to know that Billy Chadwell might well be their key to rounding up the James-Younger Gang. Ol' Billy would be receiving word from Charlie sometime in the future just before the whole James-Younger Gang aimed to pull off its biggest bank job ever someplace up north, north of the Mason-Dixon, a job so big they all believed it would make them rich. If the Pinkertons staked out Billy Chadwell, the unwitting Billy would one day lead them straight to an unsuspecting James-Younger Gang.

The ride back to Westport and then on up to Kansas City was a quick one, Westport being just south of the newer bustling city. Bill had no more than turned his horse onto Main Street when he was gobsmacked by seeing Cole Younger himself window shopping at a local jewelry store with a "closed" sign hanging on its front door. Bill couldn't believe the coincidence of seeing Charlie Pitts, Billy Chadwell, and now Cole Younger all on the same night.

Charlie and Cole had been covered in road dust and were carrying saddlebags which they both held onto a little too tightly. Bill's years as a Union spy had trained him to look for such clues. It was clear to Bill that these men were on the run and that they had just pulled off a job somewhere in Missouri and not so far away. According to Billy, ol' Charlie had been loose with his money, tossing around twenty-dollar gold coins without a care.

The more he thought about it, a posse would never suspect these outlaws to show up walking the streets in Kansas City or Westport since the towns were crawling with Pinkerton agents and local law enforcement. Things were booming and the last thing the railroad or local merchants wanted were outlaws shooting up Main Street. On second thought, hiding in plain sight was not such a bad idea for these notorious desperadoes. He had done it more than once during the war.

Bill decided he would find a place to stay for the night and come back to the jewelry store in the morning before heading to his scheduled meeting with Mr. Jeffers at the Kansas City stockyard. He needed to know what Cole was up to. More importantly, he needed to know where Cole was headed next.

May 4, 1867

Kansas City, Jackson County, Missouri

Wedding Belle Dreams

BILL, CLEAN-SHAVEN AND IN fresh clothes, walked up the boardwalk on Main Street. Blending in with other townsfolk, he walked as though he had lived there his whole life. Without fanfare he stopped in at the jewelry store where he had seen Cole the night before. Entering the store, he nearly bumped into Cole Younger himself who was standing at a counter near the door, discussing a large diamond ring with the jeweler.

The jeweler was holding up the ring, twisting it between his fingers as Cole studied how the ring's magnificent multifaceted stone caught the morning light coming in through the front window of the shop. Cole, with his attention fixed on the sparkling diamond ring when Bill entered the shop, paid no mind to the presence of a faceless customer, his sole focus on the ring and his business with the jeweler.

"So how much did you say this one would run?" Cole said, seeming to weigh the advantages of one ring over another.

"This stone came all the way from the Vaal in South Africa, sir. These diamonds are the latest rage in London and Paris, sir. I could let you have it for no less than five thousand dollars, sir," the jeweler said, placing the ring onto the small piece of black velvet he had spread out on the glass countertop.

If asked, neither man would have been able to tell anyone what or where the Vaal was, even the jeweler from whose lips the strange-sounding name had flowed like honey. All that both men knew for certain was that the precious gem had come from a mysterious land somewhere in the depths of the dark continent somewhere on the other side of the world. Transfixed, they gazed at the sparkling diamond, clearly in awe.

Cole was not accustomed to shopping for expensive jewelry and had no idea how to measure the ring's value. "That seems steep for a little ol' gold and platinum band and a shiny stone," he said, not taking his eyes off the diamond ring that seemed to float of its own accord above a carpet of jet-black velvet.

"It is a one-of-a-kind stone, sir, with excellent color, clarity, and a flawless cut, sir. This is Kansas City, sir, not New York City, sir, to have this quality of a gemstone this far west is unprecedented, sir. Your bride will be the envy of every woman this side of the Mississippi, sir," the jeweler exclaimed, clearly frustrated that Cole was unable to truly appreciate the value of the diamond's flawless cut or the artistry of its matchless setting or even its overall exquisite beauty. The ring, the jeweler clearly felt, was the finest he had ever had the privilege to put on sale.

"Can I have the inside of the band engraved?" Cole asked, picking up the ring to look at the inside of its band.

"Absolutely sir, it is part of our service, sir. Just let me know what you would like to have engraved and I can have it ready for you first thing tomorrow morning, sir," the jeweler said, taking the ring back from Cole to study the inside of the band.

"Alright then, I'll take it," Cole said as he offered his hand to the jeweler.

After the two men shook hands, the jeweler said, "Excellent, sir. And the engraving? What would you like it to read, sir?"

Tipping his hat back, Cole looked at the jeweler like a little boy afraid to tell his mother the truth. A long uncomfortable silence held the two men in limbo, the jeweler unwilling to speak and Cole unable to do so. Finally, the silence was broken. "I would like it to say, "Two Hearts Beating as One,"" Cole said with a quiver in his voice, as though he was embarrassed to say the words out loud for the first time in his life.

"A beautiful sentiment, sir," the jeweler said, both surprised and relieved. "I am sure the young lady will be thrilled, sir. I will have the ring engraved and ready for pick-up by seven o'clock tomorrow morning, sir. Now, how would you like to pay, sir?" the jeweler continued, wanting to quickly get down to business.

"Cash be alright?" Cole said as he reached into his saddlebags and counted out five thousand dollars in cash and gold coins onto the jeweler's counter.

"Cash will be just fine, sir, just fine, sir," the jeweler said in the politest tone of voice he could manage as he gathered up the large stacks of bills and coins, fighting hard to keep his hands from shaking.

"Alright then, I'll be here first thing tomorrow morning to pick up the ring. You just be damn sure it's ready, I plan on gettin' hitched tomorrow without delay," Cole said, looking the jeweler square in the eye. The jeweler suddenly realized Cole was not just another customer; the look he found in Cole's eyes told him that he was looking into the eyes of the Reaper himself, the eyes of a stone-cold killer.

"It will be ready, sir. There will be no delay, sir," the jeweler reassured Cole as beads of sweat visibly formed across his brow and upper lip.

"Just understand, there'll be hell to pay if there's any delay. Comprende?" Cole said with a subtle growl in his voice, still holding his eyes fixed on the jeweler.

"Yes, yes, certainly, sir. It will be ready first thing tomorrow morning, sir. No delays, sir, no delays" the jeweler ventured, his head nodding up and down in affirmation with every word as rivulets of sweat now visibly ran down his forehead.

Cole pulled the brim of his hat back down and touched it with a nod. "Till tomorrow mornin' then," Cole said. His business completed, he turned quickly and left the jewelry store without looking back.

Bill now knew what Cole was up to. He also knew he had little time to spare if he hoped to stay ahead of the swiftly-moving events unfolding before him. Cole's desire to marry Lucy as soon as possible had changed Bill's plans. Bill and Lucy had no time to steal off to California in a few months or try any number of other options that would take time to set up. He would have to ride back to Buchanan County as soon as he wrapped up his business at the stockyard to have any hope of staying ahead of Cole Younger's fast-moving wedding plans. Bill knew he had no time to dally.

Once he got back to Buchanan County, Bill would have to convince Lucy that Cole was on his way and that they must make a run for it without delay. Bill thought their only option now was to head north to hide out back at his place on Lizard Creek. Bill's mind raced as he worked out his new plan on the fly. Since none of the James-Younger Gang knew where he came from and the Youngers had no idea what he looked like, such a plan might work. Lucy would have to stay out of sight at least for a while. Wilber, Nancy, and their kids could be recruited to help.

Bill knew Cole would set out for Buchanan County as soon as he had the ring in hand, Bill and Lucy would need to ride out of Buchanan County late tonight or, if delayed, early tomorrow morning at the very latest. It would be close, but if all went well, they could be in Iowa long before Cole reached the Little Platte.

Bill remained in the shop pretending to admire a display case full of turquoise and silver jewelry while he watched Cole march up the street in the mirror-like reflection of the display case glass. Satisfied the coast was clear, Bill turned to leave the shop.

"May I help you, sir?" the jeweler inquired, as he dabbed sweat off his forehead and upper lip, the five-thousand-dollar smile Cole had put on his face once again firmly in place.

"No, I think I got everything I needed," Bill said as he stepped out onto the boardwalk.

The jeweler was far too giddy from making the sale of a lifetime to wonder what the faceless customer might have meant by his remark. Without skipping a beat, and knowing somehow his life depended on it, he picked up the two-carat diamond ring and quickly headed for his engraving bench in the back of the shop.

As Cole walked up the boardwalk, no one seemed the wiser as to his identity. He was convinced if he could only get to California with his lovely Lucy-belle, they would be able to start a new life, one where he would no longer need to constantly look over his shoulder for the law closing in.

As he made his way back to his hotel, he recalled his last encounter with his Lucy-belle now over two months ago.

"Now, Cole, I have to get back home," Lucy protested as she struggled in vain to pull away from Cole's vise-like embrace.

"Just a little longer, Lucy-belle. Now give me another one of those sweet, sweet kisses of yours," Cole said in a tender voice.

Lucy yield to Cole as they kissed, his tongue probing her lips until she opened her mouth to him. After spooning for several minutes, Cole's kisses became more impassioned, his breathing more irregular. Lucy, caught up in the moment, soon felt his rough hands rove across her soft bare skin. Minutes passed until she realized her blouse had been ripped open, her breasts laid bare to Cole's eager mouth and tongue. His lust for her became like a runaway freight train with Lucy helpless to stop it or slow it down. His muscles rippled as he took her body into his hard-calloused hands. It happened quickly, the pain sharp and sudden. When it was over, Lucy lay exhausted and in shock as Cole rolled off her, sweating profusely.

Coming to her senses, Lucy realized what had happened. She sudden become ashamed and afraid, not sure how to react. "I must get home. Pappy will wonder where I've been," Lucy said anxiously, holding back her tears as she struggled to pull her blouse closed and get up.

"Settle down, Lucy-belle, there's no need to hurry on home. Pappy and I have an agreement. He knows you're with me and he knows you're my woman now," Cole said firmly as he grabbed her blouse, ripping it open and causing her to fall back down beside him. Once again, he pinned her to the ground tightly as he pressed his sweat-drenched hairy chest hard against her smooth bare breasts and took her a second time. Her bloomers already ripped open and her dress hiked up around her waist had made it impossible for Lucy to resist his brutish strength. In pain Lucy groaned out, causing Cole to finish quickly. In Cole's mind, he had heard Lucy moan in pleasure, the way he liked a woman to moan. He looked forward to a lifetime of making love to the beautiful Lucy Breeden.

Before they parted, he kissed her passionately with a lingering kiss unlike any he had given to any woman in his life. As their lips parted, he looked into Lucy's eyes and though he saw only fear and confusion, he imagined their hearts beating together as one. It was at that moment that he realized how deeply he felt for her. For Cole, now that they had made love, Lucy-belle was his woman, and in time he was certain, her girlish confusion would fade and her womanly love for him would grow. One day, she would come to accept that he was her man. The only man she would ever have.

Cole saw himself as the gentle yet firm lover and his Lucy-belle as his seemingly reluctant though willing partner. He had always believed a woman liked a firm hand and a strong man and that it was more shyness and embarrassment than anything else that made a woman pretend to resist the advances of her man. It was because of his growing love for Lucy-belle that he had his deepest secret feelings for her etched into the band of the wedding ring he planned to surprise her with. He wanted desperately for his Lucy-belle to feel as deeply for him as he felt for her.

He had lost his first love when his best friend married her. He had come to accept that Belle Shirley never really loved him and had bedded many a man including his own brother Jim. Lucy-belle had come to eclipse Belle Shirley's fading memory and she was now the only woman he desired. He truly believed with every fiber of his being that their hearts were meant to beat forever as one and that he would kill any man who tried to come between them.

When Bill arrived at the stockyards before nine o'clock, he was a man without any time to waste. Entering the main offices, Mr. Theodor Jeffers had already taken up the head chair at a large mahogany table in an oak-paneled meeting room to the right of the reception counter.

"Good morning Mr. Thompson, good to have you here on time," Mr. Jeffers said as he greeted Bill and motioned for him to take up a seat. "The others will arrive soon and then we can get down to business. Thank you again for an enjoyable evening in Westport."

"Good morning Mr. Jeffers, no need to thank me, I always enjoy a good meal at Delmonico's. I hope you had a restful evening," Bill said, never very good at small talk.

"Yes, frontier life can be exciting. As I told you, this is my first trip this far west," Mr. Jeffers said with more than a little excitement in his voice.

"Good morning, gentlemen," Fred Larson boomed as he stepped into the room. "I've checked with the yard and all is in order," he added as he took a seat at the table.

Fred had no more than sat down when a man and a woman both in business attire entered the room carrying leather satchels.

"Good morning, everyone. My name is Victor McMillen. I will be representing the Commerce Bank this morning, and this is Miss Susana Elverson, my assistant. We have all the necessary documents and bank drafts with us. Just a matter of filling in the particulars," Victor said with professional aplomb as the two took their seats.

"Thank you. Thank you. Well, it seems everybody is here and ready to get down to business. Let's get started," Jeffers said, looking at Bill.

"I take it our agreed price was thirty dollars a head," Bill said looking back at Mr. Jeffers.

"And how many animals are there?" Jeffers said, looking at Fred Larson.

"As of an hour ago the head count was four-hundred ninety-eight. Now, now, Mr. Thompson, don't be upset, I know you had five hundred head when you brought the herd in three weeks ago. Losing a couple of penned-up animals is not unusual. We'll split the loss with you and adjust your stockyard bill accordingly. I hope this is agreeable with all parties," Fred said, looking at Bill intently at first and then looking back and forth between the two men.

Both men nodded their agreement. "Very well then, I'm prepared to pay twenty-six dollars a head for the remaining cattle. This I think is only fair since there is no telling how many more animals may be lost before they reach St. Louis. My investors cannot accept these kinds of losses," Mr. Jeffers said, pulling sharply on the lapels of his suit, as he stiffened his spine and sat back from the table with his hands folded in front of him.

The room fell silent as everyone waited for Bill's response. Negotiating a lower price was customary; however, cutting the price by four dollars a head from the already low price of thirty dollars a head would be unheard of. Everyone in the room knew Bill might get more than thirty-two or even thirty-five dollars a head if he held out for more bids. The prices for prime beef back east were soaring.

"You've got yourself a deal, Mr. Jeffers. Twenty-six dollars a head," Bill relented, knowing he had no time to haggle and no time to find another offer. Mr. Jeffers was the only fish he had on his line and one sucker he wasn't about to let slip the hook. That the law might be closing in was also a factor that couldn't be ignored.

"Wonderful, just wonderful," Jeffers exclaimed, almost jumping out of his chair with excitement. He had just pocketed another two thousand dollars in profits by cutting the price by four dollars a head. His investors would be thrilled.

Surprised by the sudden conclusion of negotiations and the final low price per head, Victor McMillen, maintaining his professional demure and with the assistance of Miss Elverson, helped Mr. Jeffers and Mr. Thompson fill out the proper paperwork for the transfer of title to the cattle to Mr. Jeffers and the payment of nearly 13,000 dollars to Mr. Thompson.

Fred Larson in the meantime worked on totaling up Mr. Thompson's stockyard fees as of that day. At two-bits a day per animal for twenty-one days, plus additional miscellaneous charges, the total bill came to over three-thousand dollars, even after figuring in the loss of the two animals.

When Fred announced the total due, Bill received the news without complaint. Rather than go over each charged item with Fred as was the customary practice, he accepted Fred's tally as written. Turning once again to the surprised Mr. McMillen, Bill asked him to draw up the proper payment papers to settle with the stockyard as soon as payment for the cattle had been completed. After settling accounts at the stockyard and completing the transfer of title to the cattle, Bill accompanied Mr. McMillon and the lovely Miss Elverson to the bank, where without fanfare, he requested the remaining balance be paid to him in cash. He also requested that any funds in his current bank account be withdrawn in cash and that the account be closed.

When the dust settled a little over two hours after setting down at the table at the Kansas City stockyards with Mr. Theodor Jeffers, Bill walked out of the Commerce Bank with over 35,000 dollars in his saddlebags, a small fortune for any man. Cashing out his ill-gotten gains from the past couple of years by closing his bank account had been in many ways his symbolic act of killing and burying his alter ego Leroy Thompson once and for all. With thoughts of Lucy and their future ever on his mind, he was determined to put his outlaw days behind him.

Seeking a reassuring sign, Bill scanned the sky as he walked up the boardwalk. Sun dogs flanked the midday fiery ball of the sun and nipped at its heels as it slowly slid toward the distant western horizon. Sun dogs had always been harbingers of change, though not always for the better, he thought. Bill took their pursuit of the sun as an ill omen, fearing they confirmed that he and Lucy were headed into a life on the run.

May 4, 1867

Little Platte, Buchanan County, Missouri

Without Mercy

BILL RODE NORTH OUT of Kansas City with his saddlebags bulging with ill-gotten money and several sacks of candies for Wilber and Nancy's growing herd. Bringing back sweets for his nieces and nephews was a small thing, but considering all his troubles and concerns, it brought a smile to his face to think about how they would go wild over all the lemon drops, saltwater taffy, and peppermint sticks. Trailing behind him was a fully outfitted strawberry roan he had bought for Lucy. If he and Lucy were going to make a run for it, they would both need good horseflesh under them. He arrived in Buchanan County in the late afternoon. Lucy had told him where she lived and how to get there. He decided to approach the main cabin from the rear to avoid making any undue commotion or alerting anyone of his arrival. He hoped with luck, he would be able to find Lucy alone and that no one else would know he was in the area.

Staking the horses nearby in a shallow ravine with plenty of grass and a small free-running spring, he worked his way slowly up to the back of the cabin. Lucy was nowhere to be seen. Scanning the nearby woods, he noticed a shadowy figure moving through the trees. Bill froze as the figure grew closer. It wasn't until the figure rounded the last clump of low-lying bushes that he recognized it was Lucy Breeden. She was as beautiful as ever, her hair flowing behind her, bouncing with every step she took. She walked as if unaware of her beauty or that anyone would ever take notice of it.

Bill moved out into the open where she would be able to see him and motioned with both arms to get her attention. "Lucy, over here," Bill said, trying to keep his voice low not knowing who might be inside the cabin or how he might be greeted.

Lucy was startled until she saw that it was Bill and quickly joined him behind the cabin. "Why are you back here so soon?" Lucy said, her face etched with concern.

Moving back behind the cabin, Bill told Lucy about what he had witnessed at the jewelry shop in Kansas City. There was no doubt that as soon as Cole picked up the diamond wedding ring in the morning, he would be headed straight to Pappy's cabin to fetch his bride-to-be. Hearing the news, Lucy was shocked and frightened.

She told Bill how it was only yesterday evening that Pappy had told her that he had received a telegram delivered by an unknown messenger from Cole Younger requesting Lucy's hand in marriage, and that Cole had offered to pay five thousand dollars as a bride price. There was no way Pappy would be able to turn Cole's offer down. Cole and his bloodthirsty brothers would take Lucy from him either way, dead or alive. Pappy had decided he would have to take the money and Lucy would have to agree to marry Cole. If she didn't, Cole might kill them both. Pappy's hope was that Lucy might be able to escape Cole's grip in the future, and if she did, he would have the money they would need to make a run for it. It was no consolation, but it was all he had to offer. Pappy was no gunslinger and with no other living kin in the area to back him up, he had no way to stop Cole from doing whatever he wanted. By the time she finished her story, her eyes had filled with tears as she looked to Bill for comfort.

"Pappy's right. Making a run for it is the only way to come out of this alive," Bill said with conviction. "We need to leave tonight," he added, never more certain of anything in his life. "Is there any way you can throw a bag of your things out a back window? I will gather everything up and ready the horses. They're posted in the shallow ravine just beyond that grove of hickory trees," he continued, pointing to the stand of hickory trees near a small pole barn at the edge of the clearing. Bill had worked out an escape plan and needed Lucy to get onboard.

"We should tell Pappy. He could help," Lucy said, starting to move toward the front of the cabin.

"No. You can't tell him," Bill said as he grabbed her shoulders and looked her square in the eyes. "The less he knows, the more likely he'll survive Cole's wrath."

"What do you mean? Pappy can help us escape," Lucy insisted, pulling her shoulders away.

"Believe me, the less he knows, the better off he'll be. Pappy needs to be as surprised as everyone else that you ran off without his knowledge or consent," Bill said, trying to make the situation clear to her. "If Cole suspects even for a second that Pappy had a hand in your escape, he'll kill him on the spot," he said flatly.

"Oh my God. What should we do?" Lucy said, hoping there was an answer.

"The best course is to act natural when you spend time with Pappy this evening. Keeping Pappy in the dark will be tough, but in the end, it may be the only thing that saves his life," Bill said as he looked into Lucy's eyes, pleading with her for understanding.

"I understand," she agreed as she brought her emotions under control. "Pappy goes to bed a couple of hours after supper. He's the only one in the cabin. My window is the one on the left. I'll shove some things out first chance I get. I'll sneak out as soon as Pappy is asleep," she said as she wiped her eyes, her face never more serious.

She knew this was the only way. Even if she told Pappy, there was no telling how he might respond. She also knew he would never agree to run off with them and leave his life's work behind for an uncertain future. Pappy had very little money and was too old to start over. The best course was for Lucy to escape Cole's grip and pray Pappy survived his wrath. Pappy's best chance was to be as shocked and confused as everyone else about Lucy's sudden disappearance.

Before long the night air grew colder as Bill sat crouched on a short stump in the shadows of the tree line along the back of the cabin. True to her word, Lucy had pushed a bundle of her things out the cabin window and Bill had quickly gathered it up and tied it to her horse. Bill was certain everything was now in place for a quick escape.

As he waited for Lucy to join him, Bill chewed on a supper of cold hardtack and biscuits he had picked up from an outfitter in Independence before crossing the Missouri River. A large barn owl on a branch somewhere high above him made a series of harsh scream-like calls into the darkness before swooping to a tree deeper in the wood. Bill's mind drifted as he thought about the best trail north and home. While his mind pondered one thing and then another, he came upon on a question for which he had no answer. Who was Cole Younger's messenger? Who had told Pappy to make

Lucy ready for Cole's arrival? Lucy said the telegram had been delivered by an unknown messenger. It seemed unlikely the messenger was one of Cole's brothers. It must be somebody from around these parts, somebody keeping an eye on Cole Younger's sweetheart.

In the sudden rush of events, Lucy had forgotten to warn Bill about Molly B. Bill, however, had arrived at his own conclusions about Molly B long before returning to Buchanan County. He had no doubt the mountain she-bear was in cahoots with Cole Younger. Bill also now believed she was more than likely Cole's messenger and possibly much more than that.

Bill wondered if Molly B knew about him and Lucy or if she might already know he was in the area. It seemed unlikely she would suspect him back in Buchanan County to see Lucy so soon, knowing he had headed to Westport less than two days ago supposedly to join a wagon train headed west. Just the same, Bill checked his pistol and slid down off the stump to cut down on any silhouette he might be showing. He scanned the area looking for any movement or anything out of place. The hair on the back of his neck bristled from an eerie feeling that he was not alone.

Suddenly, Lucy bolted from the front of the cabin and started running toward him while trying to avoid making noise. Out of the shadows Lucy was met by a huge dark menacing form that stopped her dead in her tracks.

"Where ya goin' so fast, ya little hussy?" Molly B's voice rang out as she collared the fleeing maiden.

Wasting no time, Bill sprang from his hiding place under the trees and charged across the short distance to where Molly B had Lucy throttled. Running at full speed, Bill leaped at the last moment, ramming his right knee deep into the square of Molly B's back. Landing behind her, he threw all his weight behind punches with his hammer-hard balled-up fists into Molly B's kidneys, first on one side and then on the other. His punches hit home, taking Molly B by surprise as she gave out a screeching howl. Bill knew she would be pissing blood for a week from the damage he had inflicted. Molly B's grip on Lucy momentarily loosened, allowing Lucy, kicking and punching, to break free.

Molly B, still stunned by Bill's unexpected blows from behind, sought to regain the advantage. Bill knew if he gave her a half chance to recover, he would have to shoot her and probably more than once to put her down. In a fair fight, Molly B had the strength to tear any man apart, limb from limb. She turned quicker than Bill expected and soon had him in a crushing bear hug. Bill, holding his pistol like a hammer, slammed its butt down on the top of her head with incredible force. The blow sent a cracking sound out into the night but seemed to have no effect as the muscles in her mighty arms tightened, coiling around him like a python in a crushing death grip. Dizzy with pain, Bill fought desperately to break free.

On the verge of blacking out, he continued hammering her skull relentlessly, blow after blow, until finally she went down on both knees. Pushing himself free of her limp arms, Bill stumbled backward, his ribcage screaming in pain as he struggled to catch his breath. Looking at the massive hulk in front of him, he could see that Molly B was panting heavily, her head hanging down with blood oozing out of multiple gashes. As she shook her head from side to side, she pulled out a small whistle from a pocket in her buckskin jacket. She quickly raised it to her lips and blew with every ounce of breath she could manage. A high-pitched piercing sound ripped through the curtain of darkness in all directions. Bill immediately knew what this meant. She had called in her hounds. Whether on four legs or two he had no doubt they were on their way.

Her head still hanging down, she continued to shake it hard, trying to ready herself for a second round. Before she could gather her strength, without mercy, Bill kicked her square in the face as hard as he could, knocking her and her front teeth completely out, leaving her a crumpled heap on the ground. Knowing they had no time to waste, Bill ran with Lucy to the horses. Without looking back, they mounted their horses, turned them to the north, and rode off into the night.

Awakened by Molly B's screeching whistle, Pappy had come running out of his cabin with his double-barreled shotgun at the ready. By the time Pappy discovered what had happened, Lucy was long gone. Finding Molly B sprawled out on the ground, her mouth a toothless hole and her head a bloody pulp, he knew that when Cole arrived, there would be hell to pay.

Swallowed up by the darkness, Bill and Lucy had ridden no more than a half mile when Bill felt a searing pain slice across his left arm, followed almost immediately by the distinctive retort of a Winchester rifle at close range. Catching the barrel flare out of the corner of his eye, Bill quickly pulled out his Colt and fired three shots into the shadows, one into where the flare had come from and one on each side. Pulling up his horse and dismounting in a single move, he began running zigzag in the direction of his intended target.

"Bushwhackers!" Bill yelled as he ran. "Lucy, pull up and get off your horse! Get down behind somethin'!"

Lucy quickly reined up her horse and dismounted. She then pulled her horse down on his side and laid down behind him. Her father had taught her the old cavalry move long ago. She had never expected it might one day save her life.

Bill quickly covered the ground between the main trail and where he had first seen the barrel flare. Moving slowly on cat's feet, Bill creeped up inch by inch closer to the spot. Hearing a twig snap to his left, without hesitation, Bill tucked and rolled, coming up firing into the bushes from where the sound had come.

"Stop shooting, damn it! Please stop!" a young voice called out.

Before making his reply, Bill quickly reloaded his pistol. "Come out with your hands high!" Bill called out. "Any sudden moves and I'll cut you down where you stand."

"I can't come out, you done kilt me. I'm gut shot all to hell," the young-er voice whimpered. "Help me mister, I'm thirsty. Please I'm dyin."

Easing his way closer, Bill could see a youngster sprawled out in the tall grass, holding his stomach which looked to be drenched in blood. "Who else is with you?" Bill said through clinched teeth.

"No one, I swear. Molly B paid me twenty dollars to shoot any man trying to ride out of the Breeden place tonight. We heard her whistle," the boy said and then realizing his mistake, quickly adding, "I mean, me and my hoss Sandy over there, we heard her whistle and came runnin." Suspect-ing the boy was lying, Bill pretended to believe every word.

"Let me get you some water, son. We can take a look at that wound. Here, let me help you up," Bill said loudly, stepping on fallen branches and dried leaves, making no effort to cover his movements as he eased closer to the boy. He could see that it was the boy's right arm that had been badly wounded and that he was holding it over his stomach to make it appear he had been gut-shot. He could also see the boy was trying to hide a knife in his left hand but figured he would be able to easily overpower the scrawny kid if necessary. His bigger concern was a second shooter.

Making noise to draw attention to himself, he tried to convince any possible second shooter he had let down his guard. In doing so, Bill was playing a dangerous game. Bill gambled that if there was another shooter, he would be emboldened to make his play now. Just as Bill stepped forward, instead of making himself a clear target he unexpectedly dove down beside the boy and quickly pushed the boy's body up in front of his own, a trick he had learned during the war.

"Hey, what the hell," the boy cried out in surprise, his left hand holding a Bowie knife now pointed high into the air and in the wrong direction away from Bill. Just then, rifle shots rang out from nearby, the boy's body catching the two bullets meant for Bill. As the hot lead slugs drilled into the boy's body, the boy dropped the knife and gave out a primal scream as his life raced out of him.

Using the boy's lifeless body as a shield, Bill fired back, drawing more fire from the tree stand nearby. The boy's body took the full brunt of the close-range rifle blasts as Bill watched for barrel flares to help him hone in on where the second bushwhacker was dug in. Bill's mind raced for a solution. Using an old tree branch lying next to the boy, Bill propped up his lifeless body like a scarecrow and slid off on his belly using the boy's silhouette to cover his moves. More shots ripped into the boy's body as Bill circled around behind the hidden bushwhacker. Silence reigned as a stiff breeze raked its way through the surrounding tree branches, making them creak as they swayed back and forth. Bill soon found himself directly behind the crouched gunman. Unaware he had been flanked, the bushwhacker continued to sight down his rifle to the spot where the boy's riddled body still hung, propped up on the broken tree branch.

Holding his pistol with both hands, Bill held the bushwhacker square in his sights before shouting, "Drop your rifle!" The startled bushwhacker froze for an instant until he quickly turned to fire. His move was lighting fast, but not near fast enough. Bill's Colt barked four times before the bushwhacker could make a full turn. Dead midturn, the bushwhacker's Winchester fired once straight into the air in a kind of single gun salute leaving only an expression of utter surprise forever etched into the highway man's lifeless face.

Without checking the bodies or caring what happened to them next, Bill called out for Lucy. "Lucy! Are you alright?" his voice urgent.

"Oh Bill, I'm fine. Is it over?" Lucy called back. "Are you alright?" she urgently added.

"Yes, it was a close call, but I'm fine," he replied, still out of breath.

"I thought I recognized the voice of the bushwhacker who cried out. I think it was Joey McKenzie," Lucy continued, her emotions running high.

"Who's Joey?" Bill asked, reloading his pistol as he made his way back over to Lucy.

"He was the youngest of the McKenzie brothers who live in these parts. He runs with his older brother Ethan," Lucy said, now certain these were the two men Bill had just killed.

"More'n likely, they were Molly B's henchmen," Bill said flatly. "She probably hired local boys to cover her back trail. They were good, but not professionals. They both paid the price for that," he added without emotion. Considering the bullet-riddled and gory condition in which he left their bodies, Bill figured the bushwhackers' kin would be looking to even the score. The last thing Bill needed now was a feud with a vengeful McKenzie clan.

"They were the last of the McKenzies," Lucy said almost to herself as the realization of who the bushwhackers were struck her hard.

"What do you mean, last of the McKenzies?" Bill asked, surprised Lucy seemed to know what he had been thinking.

"Those two men were Joey and Ethan McKenzie, the youngest of the five McKenzie boys. They had three older brothers who joined the Confederacy together and fought and died together at the Battle of Chickamauga in September 1863," Lucy said. "Just like my own brothers, Robert and Lynsey, who ran off and fought and died together for the Union at the Battle of Spotsylvania in May 1864 during Grant's Overland Campaign," Lucy added with a quiver in her voice.

"There were too many good men who died on both sides during the war. When you take a man's life, you leave him with nothing more to give," Bill said as memories of the war filled his mind.

"It seems unbelievable, but the McKenzies' pa and ma both died during the same scarlet fever epidemic that took my ma and so many of our neighbors in the fall of 1864. Our families have been bound by a chain of endless misery since the secession of the South. The war years have been damn hard on folks in these parts. And now, the last two McKenzie boys are just as dead as all the rest of 'em," Lucy said shaking her head as she wiped tears from her eyes.

She had known the McKenzie family since childhood. The break between the Breeden and McKenzie families had come when they found their loyalties on opposite sides of the Civil War, a fate faced by many once neighborly families in the border states. Now, the McKenzies had all been swept away as if they had never walked the face of the earth.

Lucy's outpouring of sorrow for all the senseless deaths brought home to Bill the gravity of the enormous losses families all over the nation had suffered in recent years. During the war and the years that followed, Bill had done his share of killing. He was not proud of it. He had killed when he had to kill. He hoped these two men would be the last he would add to his mounting tally.

The war had taken a terrible toll on both sides. The total number of casualties had ballooned with every news report since the end of the war. For every man killed on the battlefield, two more had died of disease. Bill had read only recently that over 600,000 soldiers had died in the war, not to mention the countless wounded, many losing limbs, or worse, losing their minds. The death toll among the civilian population including his own family back in Illinois would never be completely known. In the South and the border states of Missouri, Kentucky, Delaware and Maryland, one in four men who joined the fight for the Confederacy never returned home. Both sides often recruited regiments numbering a thousand men strong from several adjacent counties, making the impact on local communities especially devastating should the local regiment suffer heavy battle casualties.

Brothers and close kin fighting together was common during the war which further increased the impact of heavy losses on families. This seems to have been the fate of the three McKenzie brothers who had fought and died together in the same Confederate regiment formed up in western Tennessee of border state volunteers from Kentucky and Missouri. A similar fate had been suffered by the two Breeden brothers who had run off to join the same Union regiment made up largely of border state volunteers that had been formed up in western Ohio.

Lucy reached out for Bill and he took her into his arms. They embraced in the middle of the road and held each other tight, their two hearts beating as one. Though Bill had no idea how many more men Molly B might have hired, he figured she wasn't one to waste money. These two yahoos were more than likely the only ones she dealt into her deadly game. With the McKenzie boys now cashed out of the game, Bill's immediate concern was getting the hell out of Missouri before Cole Younger had the chance to deal himself in.

Lucy felt safe in Bill's arms. Having witnessed the quickness of his actions and his toughness in dealing with Molly B and the McKenzie boys, she now saw Bill in a new light. She knew he had fought in the war, but she had no idea Bill had the sand to take on Molly B, let alone bushwhacking gunmen, head on. She knew Bill would be no match for Cole Younger and his brothers, but she felt a damn sight better about their chances, knowing Bill could fight like a lion and handle a gun when the chips were down. Though she was proud of how Bill had responded to the surprise ambush, she was left with a nagging question of what else she might not know about the increasingly mysterious Bill Barton. She knew she loved him more than life itself. She was unsure, however, that she knew who he really was.

Standing in the middle of the trail in each other's arms, Bill and Lucy froze when they heard the sliding metallic click of a Winchester rifle's distinctive lever action pull a fresh cartridge into its firing chamber. Realizing too late that there was a third bushwhacker, Bill cursed himself for underestimating Molly B. He should have guessed she would have hired an extra gun for a little extra insurance.

"Well, well, quite the lovebirds! Now Bill, or whatever the hell your name is, drop that gun belt right where you stand," a man's voice barked from the shadows behind Bill and Lucy.

Bill knew the man had got the drop on them. They had no choice but to do as he said.

"Mister Henny! What? Why?" Lucy said, shocked as the form of a man she had known since childhood slowly emerged out of the shadows. John Henny and Pappy had been neighbors and good friends for many years, pitching in on each other's places when the work required more than one man. Old man Henny had been a good-natured friend to the Breeden family for as long as Lucy could remember. For Lucy, to believe old man Henny was now working with Molly B against Pappy was impossible to accept.

"Molly B hired the McKenzie boys to cover this here trail. She hired me to back 'em up," Henny said, pointing his rifle directly at Bill's chest.

"I'll triple whatever she's paying ya. Just tell her you missed us. We don't want any trouble," Bill said, hoping he might negotiate with the old man long enough to figure out a way to overpower him.

"Trouble? You ain't no trouble. Your poke'll be mine soon enough, stranger. Molly B paid me a hundred dollars and promised a hundred more for the hide of any male varmint I bring her. No way I'm back out of this deal," he said with a chuckle. "Either way, I watched how ya gunned down the McKenzie boys like a couple of stray dogs. They're due a little payback, you son-of-a-bitch. Those boys were like my own blood kin."

"You know Lucy, she's a good woman. She doesn't love the outlaw Cole Younger. Why not let us go?" Bill asked, trying to buy more time.

"Women never know what's good for 'em. Lucy won't be running off with the likes of you. Her beau's Cole Younger, a true Confederate hero. I'll not be challengin' that," he said as he shifted his stance and squared his shoulders.

"Mister Henny, I love this man, not Cole. Please let us go!" Lucy said, desperate to plead with the old man's better angels. "You can't just gun him down!" Lucy demanded.

"The hell I can't," he said dryly, his features hard and full of hate.

Just as old man Henny raised his rifle to his shoulder to fire into Bill's chest, Bill dove at the old man as a shot rang out. Hitting the old man in the chest headlong, Bill rode the old man to the ground, landing, to his surprise, on the body of a dead man. Confused, Bill found himself looking into the old man's grizzled face with its eyes wide open and its features forever frozen in an expression of shock. The old man's body showed no sign of a wound other than blood oozing from his ears. Confused, Bill had no answer.

Checking his own body, he patted himself down until he was satisfied that he was in one piece and without any fresh holes. "Lucy, you alright? What the hell happened?" he said, frantically looking for answers.

Getting up, Bill looked back at Lucy and found her holding a pistol with a thin thread of gun smoke still uncoiling from its barrel. "I had to kill him, Bill. He'd have gunned ya down. I had no other choice," she said as she nodded at the old man's dead body, her emotions in check. Bill noted the look on her face was stoic and determined; it was a look he had never witnessed before, but one he was damn happy to see now.

"How? Where did you . . . " Bill stammered as he tried to gather his thoughts.

"I brought one of Pappy's pistols with me. I hadn't planned on using it, but like Pappy always says, it never hurts to be prepared," Lucy said, answering his questions before he was able put them into words.

Bill now saw Lucy in a new light and understood she was much more than just a "little sweet thing" or some innocent beauty, she was a tough frontier woman with plenty of moxie.

"Damn good thing you came prepared and can shoot straight," Bill said with a forced chuckle, still shaken by what had been a damn close call. Molly B had dealt a joker into her game and the play damn near won her the hand. Had Lucy not dealt herself into the game at the last second, it would have all ended right where they now stood.

"So, you're saying a woman can't shoot straight?" Lucy shot back, with her bottom lip turned down and her eyebrows arched up in a comical gesture of disbelief.

"Well, I think you've proved that ain't so," he said taking her back into his arms. "Now, where were we, before we were so rudely interrupted," he said as the tension drained out of their bodies. They had somehow defeated Molly B's best efforts and survived. As they held onto one another, they felt their hearts beating as one. They knew since their first embrace that this was their enduring truth, come what may.

Bill and Lucy took a moment to look into each other's eyes and then kissed deeply before turning to ready their horses for the trail ahead. In years to come, how she had put a bullet through Henny's head, perfectly in one ear and out the other, just as he was ready to fire on Bill and just as Bill leaped for him, was a question Lucy would refuse to answer. Instead, she would often just smile and say, "Only the wind knows."

Leaving old man Henny lay where he dropped, Bill surveyed the area one last time. Looking across the meadow next to the trail, he could just make out Joey McKenzie's body propped up like a scarecrow at the edge of the woods. He knew his brother Ethan's body laid nearby. Shaking his head, Bill wondered how many more men needed to die before he and Lucy would finally be able to live in peace.

Without further word, Bill and Lucy quickly mounted their horses, turned them back to the north, and spurred them into a gallop. As they rode on into a night lit up only by the thinnest sliver of a waning crescent moon, Bill couldn't help imagine how the shadowy world around them looked like something out of children's ghost story, with every bush a ghoul and every tree a giant ogre with huge jagged teeth and long sharp claws. He sought for a sign to comfort his mind, but only heard the high-pitched chirping and clicking sounds of bats and the deep-throated hoot of the great horned owl, all predators on the hunt for their evening meals. The only meaning he could divine from this midnight feeding frenzy was that, be it day or night, if you're the prey, you're always on the menu.

May 5, 1867

Sedalia, Pettis County, Missouri

Raw Deal

MR. THEODOR JEFFERS WAS proud of himself. He had ventured into the Wild West and had come back a winner. He had driven a hard bargain with the frontier ruffian Leroy Thompson and had bluffed him into taking only twenty-six dollars a head for cattle he already had sold in St. Louis for over forth-two dollars each. He and his investors stood to make a tidy profit of nearly 8,000 dollars without so much as stepping in a single cow pie, he whimsically thought as he chuckled to himself.

As he stood on the platform, stretching his legs while waiting for the train to get back underway, he looked toward the back of the train and found the local sheriff and several clearly agitated men peering and pointing into the cattle cars near the rear on the train. Before long, the troop walked back up toward Mr. Jeffers and the main platform.

As they approached, the sheriff waved a hand at Mr. Jeffers and said, "I understand you're Mr. Theodor Jeffers. I'm Ned Wilson, the sheriff of Pettis County."

Mr. Jeffers, somewhat startled and more than a little confused, said, "Why yes, Sheriff Wilson. How may I be of assistance?"

"I understand you just purchased 498 head of cattle from a Mr. Leroy Thompson yesterday in Kansas City," the sheriff said, his hands on his hips. "You might want to know that those cattle weren't Mr. Thompson's to sell," he continued.

"This can't be right. I have a legal bill of sale and the title to those animals right here in my jacket pocket. Fact is, I already have a buyer waiting in St. Louis who has requested delivery tomorrow morning," Mr. Jeffers said in as confident a tone as he could muster, not sure what was happening, but not liking the direction things were headed.

"He doesn't have any title worth the paper it's written on," Tom Sanders barked. "Sheriff, you saw how our brand had clearly been altered using a damn running iron. I demand the cattle be unloaded right now," he bellowed, clearly the rightful owner of the cattle and the leader of the small troop accompanying the sheriff.

"Now settle down Tom, let the law handle this," the sheriff said as he turned back to Jeffers.

Shocked, Jeffers could see that he had indeed stepped into a very large cow pie and that his investors wouldn't at all be thrilled. As exciting as his western adventure may have seemed, it would now end, like it had for so many other eastern greenhorns, with someone carrying off his scalp.

Back in Kansas City, Fred Larson laughed until he nearly pissed himself when he first heard the news that the cattle Mr. Theodor Jeffers brought from Mr. Leroy Thompson hadn't been Leroy's to sell.

Seems ol' Leroy was a cattle rustler and had used a running iron to change the brands on a herd of cattle he had rustled from a rancher over in Pettis County. Seems that Pettis County rancher got wind that his cattle might be on the noon train stopping at Sedalia Station and decided to have a look. After a quick inspection of the train's cattle cars, it didn't take him long to find his cattle and to figure out how his brand had been altered. He had the sheriff with him, so things went fast after that. In a nutshell, the rancher got his cattle back and Mr. Jeffers was sent packing back to St. Louis with no cattle and with a thirteen-thousand-dollar hole in his bank account.

After recounting the story to his brother Slim, they both had a good laugh. After they caught their breath, Fred couldn't help but add, "It was the damnedest, slickest swindle I've seen pulled off in a long time. Ya gotta hand it to ol' Leroy Thompson. The man has style." The last remark caused the two men to once again burst into uncontrollable laughter.

Fred and Slim had every reason to get a kick out of Jeffers' misfortune. When Fred had tallied up Leroy Thompson's yard bill, he had slipped in a couple of extra charges, 200 dollars for clerical fees and another 200 dollars for veterinary fees billed to a bogus company run by his brother. Leroy hadn't questioned Fred's tally and paid the yard bill in full, allowing Fred and Slim to pocket the bogus charges. Now that they learned Leroy was a shyster himself, Fred and Slim had no concern that their little act of larceny would ever come to light. Not to mention the two head of Leroy's cattle they had sold on the side before the Jeffers transaction. On that score, Leroy had once again accepted the loss of cattle without challenge, letting Fred and Slim off scot-free.

Later in the day, as he made his daily rounds at the stockyard, Fred thought to himself how things sometimes just have a way of working out. Of course, he thought again, sometimes they don't. The thought of the prim and proper Bostonian, Mr. Theodor Jeffers, with his tail twixt his legs slinking back to St. Louis with empty pockets and no cattle caused Fred to once again break into a belly laugh right in the middle of the stockyard. The yard hands working in the area had no idea what had suddenly come over their foreman. On the bright side they figured, at least the grouchy bastard was in a good mood for a change.

May 5, 1867

Little Platte, Buchanan County, Missouri

Chasing Shadows

WHEN COLE RODE INTO the Breeden Farm, he found Molly B sitting on the front porch of Pappy's cabin with her head wrapped in blood-soaked bandages, her face badly cut and swollen, and her lips split open and bleeding. Cole knew in an instant that his Lucy-belle was gone.

Joseph Breeden, known to everyone as Pappy, sheepishly stepped out onto the porch to greet Cole, as he reined up in front of the cabin and stepped down from his horse.

"Welcome, Cole. Damn good thing you're here. I'm afraid we have some real bad news," Pappy said as he tried to keep his voice low and under control. He knew his chances of surviving the day were, at that moment, slim to none.

"Your news seems damn clear to me, Pappy. Lucy's gone!" Cole barked, his face beet red, his body coiled like a rattler ready to strike. "Molly B, what the hell happened here?" Cole continued turning to Molly B for answers.

"It was Leroy, Leroy Thompson," Molly B sputtered through bleeding lips and broken teeth. "He clubbed me on the head and stole Lucy in the middle of the night. I tried to stop him, but . . ." she continued to mumble until Cole sharply cut her off.

"Looks to me like this Leroy Thompson character did a hell of a lot more than a little clubbing, he kicked the livin' shit out of ya, Molly B," Cole said through clenched teeth. "I thought you were a damn sight tougher hombre than that," he added, spitting out a wad of chewing tobacco that splattered across the toes of Molly B's boots. Taking the insult in stride, she made no move to wipe her boots off.

"I did everything I could to corral that little hussy," Molly B muttered through ruined teeth. "I even hired three damn good guns to bushwhack any son-of-bitch that tried to ride out of the Breeden place last night."

"How'd that work out for ya?" Cole snapped, the skin around his eyes twitching, his face ruby red.

Molly B feared answering Cole's question, but knew she had no choice and had to try to explain what happened. "We found all three of 'em shot all to hell not a half-mile from here. I don't know how he did it, Cole, but Leroy gunned all three of 'em down like dogs. The bodies of two of 'em were a godawful mess, all shot through with bullet holes," Lucy added, hoping her sorry tale might merit a degree of sympathy. She wanted Cole to understand she'd tried her best to keep Lucy from running off. Knowing Cole's violent temper, she feared his rage had already blinded him to everything but her failure. Molly B also knew of his notorious need for retribution for every wrong he felt he ever suffered.

Pappy had heard gun shots in the distance the night before and had feared the worst. Knowing he could do nothing that would change the course of events, he decided to wait until morning before investigating what might have happened. When Molly B finally came around, she told him that she had hired the McKenzie boys and ol' man Henny to cover the main trail. When none of the three men showed up to Pappy's cabin after the shootout, there was little doubt about what might have happened to them.

At first light, Pappy and Molly B had ridden to where Molly B said she thought her bushwhackers may have set up their ambush. The first thing they found was ol' man Henny's body laying at the side of the trail with a gunshot through his head. The shot had been clean, having gone in one ear and out the other. The shocked look on old man Henny's face said it all: his death had been sudden and unexpected. Pappy retrieved the brand-new Model 1866 Winchester rifle that lay next to him, noting the rifle was both cocked and loaded, though had never been fired. Across the meadow on the other side of the trail, propped up like a scarecrow, they found the bullet-riddled and blood-soaked body of Joey McKenzie. It didn't take long for Ethan McKenzie's body to be discovered nearby. Ethan was lying face up, his eyes wide open, staring into empty space. His body was ripped open by multiple gunshots fired at point-blank range. The front of his shirt was charred full of holes, having caught fire from muzzle flare. Pappy had known the McKenzie boys since their births and had watched them grow up. He knew Joey and Ethan were the youngest of five brothers and the last of the McKenzie clan. Seeing their young bloody bodies shot through with bullet holes, Pappy had cried uncontrollably, unable to hold back the pent-up sorrow over the senseless deaths of so many young men in recent years, including the deaths of his own two sons. That ol' man Henny had been willing to betray him for Molly B's blood money came as an utter shock to Pappy. With mixed emotions, he still felt John Henny was his friend as he had been for so many years. That he had died because of his betrayal of that friendship deeply saddened Pappy. Pappy would later learn that John Henny had been an active Confederate supporter who had secretly provided aid to Quantrill's Raiders and had even met Cole Younger on several occasions during the war. Henny had held an unspoken grudge against Pappy and other families in the area for their support of the Union cause, especially after the deaths of the three McKenzie boys at the Battle of Chickamauga.

Cole held up his left hand in a clear warning to Molly B to say no more. "Seeing how you found your hired guns shot to hell this morning and Lucy long gone, I'd say those worthless hillbillies you hired weren't very damn good pistoleros," Cole hissed, his temper on the verge of blowing. Molly B knew her life now hung by a thread.

"Pappy, you have anything to add to this sorry tale of woe or were you in on all of this?" Cole said, dryly turning his piercing glare at Pappy, his gun hand hovering over his six-shooter.

"Now Cole, you know we have a deal," Pappy pleaded, holding up his hands, palms out. "I got your message yesterday and I told Molly B this morning I was fine with the five-thousand-dollar bride price. That's a hell of a lot of money, Cole, and times have been tough. Ask her yourself. I'd never go back on our deal or lie to you, Cole. You gotta know that."

"Go on. Tell me what happened," Cole said, motioning for Pappy to continue.

"All I know is I was woken up by one hell of a shrill whistle outside the cabin last night and before I could get outside to see what was happenin', some no-good varmint had made hash out of Molly B and run off with my Lucy," Pappy said, his voice cracking when he uttered his daughter's name.

"Why the hell didn't you go after 'em?" Cole demanded.

"By the time I found Molly B laying on the ground and Lucy gone, I realized Lucy and that fella had already struck out into the night at a full gallop," Pappy groaned. "There was just no way to saddle up my horse quick enough to get on their trail to track them in the middle of the night," he concluded, ashamed as he looked down, shaking his head from side to side. "Just no way, Cole," he repeated as he raised his eyes to meet Cole's deadly glare.

Though Cole seethed with nearly uncontrollable rage, he knew he had to accept that Lucy was gone. From all indications, she had been taken by Leroy Thompson, a known cattle rustler and horse thief. Cole had heard the James brothers and Charlie Pitts talk about Leroy on more than one occasion. Knowing who took Lucy gave Cole hope. It would be just a matter of time before he would be able to track the son-of-a-bitch down and put him out of his misery. Feeling the weight of the two-carat diamond ring in his shirt pocket, Cole promised himself that Lucy would one day wear his diamond ring and that she would come to share with the man she loved the sentiment etched into its band.

Much to his relief, Pappy watched Cole cool down as he seemed to slowly come to accept the situation. Pappy had returned to his cabin after tending to Molly B's injuries the night before. It wasn't until first light in the morning that he had found Lucy's note.

> Pappy,
>
> I have found my true love. His name is Bill Barton. Mama would have loved him too, I just know it. He is a good and gentle man. Cole will kill him if we stay. Please forgive us for running off. Bill promised he would find a way for me to stay in touch. For now, we must run and hide. Pray for us, Pappy. We are praying for you.
>
> Love, Lucy

What confused him now was Lucy's mention of a man named Bill Barton with no mention of Leroy Thompson. Pappy thought this was very strange considering Molly B seemed certain that it was Leroy Thompson who attacked her and who had run off with Lucy. Cole also seemed to know who Leroy Thompson was and seemed to be satisfied that it was Leroy he needed to track down. Though Pappy didn't understand what it all meant, he knew he wouldn't be sharing his confusion or the name Bill Barton with Cole Younger or Molly B or anyone else. Having tossed Lucy's note into the cookstove fire just before coming out to greet Cole, Pappy was certain he was the only one of the three of them who would ever know the truth.

Molly B, suffering from a severe concussion, her head swimming in pain, couldn't believe how close she had come to getting the thousand-dollar bonus Cole promised her in his last message. Her job was simple: have Lucy ready to ride when Cole arrived. Cole had recognized Molly B would lose her $200 a month fee for watching Lucy and had promised to pay her a bonus to make it up to her. She now wondered if Cole would even be willing pay the $400 he owed her since the last time he was in Buchanan County, two months ago. As she stood on the porch weaving back and forth on wobbly legs, her dreams of joining a wagon train west and making it to Washington Territory, let alone further north to Alaska, were fading by the second.

Pappy knew it would be lonely without Lucy. She had been the light of his life and his anchor to the living since the senseless deaths of his only two sons, Robert and Lynsey, at the Battle of Spotsylvania and especially since the sudden death of his wife, Alda, not six months later during a scarlet fever epidemic that had swept through northern Missouri, taking so many of their neighbors with it. He often wondered if happier times would ever return. He would pray every day for Lucy's safety and for the day they would see each other again. He would also pray Bill Barton turned out to be as good a man as Lucy believed. He was not sure how they would send messages to one another, but he was confident Lucy would find a way.

Pappy was abruptly snapped out of his musings when he heard the sharp retort of a pistol followed by three quick pops. As if in a dream, he witnessed Molly B's head lurch back as blood sprayed from a fresh hole in the center of her forehead while the front of her body bloomed in patches of dark red with the impact of every bullet. Fearing he was next, he looked at Cole and awaited his own execution.

Cole stood stock-still, pistol in hand, staring at his handiwork. After a quick nod at Molly B's lifeless body now sprawled out on Pappy's front porch, he effortlessly popped open the cylinder of this pistol and quickly emptied the spent cartridges and reloaded. Snapping the cylinder back into place with a flick of his wrist, he holstered his pistol, turned on his heel, and mounted his horse.

"The bitch deserved it," Cole growled. "I don't cotton with failure. And hell, from the looks of her, I figured it was an act of mercy to put the bitch out of her misery. Take care of her stinking carcass and keep any gold coins you might find tucked away on her. Consider it a down payment on the bride price," Cole snarled. "I'll be back this way from time to time. No tellin' when. If you hear from Lucy, I want to know, comprende?" he continued his eyes spitting fire as he stared at Pappy, giving him no doubt that the consequences would be fatal should he fail to comply.

Pappy, drawing on every ounce of courage he could scrape up, met Cole's stare head-on. "We have a deal, Cole. I'll keep my end," Pappy said as confidently as he could muster.

"And I'll keep mine," Cole replied. "You'll get your five thousand dollars when I get my bride," Cole added, his words as frigid as the tone of his voice.

With that, he looked back over at Molly B's lifeless body sprawled out on the porch and then back at Pappy. Turning his horse with a flick of the reins, he rode out of Pappy's place without so much as a fare-thee-well.

August 7, 1869

Lizard Creek, Webster County, Iowa

Darkest Before the Dawn

AFTER THEIR MIDNIGHT FLIGHT into Iowa, Bill and Lucy had stayed close to home. They kept a sharp lookout for any sign of a Younger in the area and had enlisted Wilber and his ever-growing tribe to keep an eye out for strangers. Though over two years had passed with no sign of pursuit, Lucy and Bill knew the Youngers could ride in at any moment. Bill had grown more domesticated since the birth of little Johnny. The boy had grown by leaps and bounds and was their treasure, born nine months to the day after their arrival in Lizard Creek. He was christened John Oromal Barton to honor his grandfather, Oromal Bingham Barton, who had died during the war back in Illinois. Bill had wanted his father's name to live on in the boy, for he was certain that one day, John Barton would continue the family's journey west.

Bill was already in the yard, when Lucy came out of the house cradling Alda in her arms with Johnny, holding onto her apron, walking at her side. Johnny's little sister, Alda Roberta-Lyn Barton, had been born only the month before and had been named to honor Lucy's mother, Alda, and her brothers, Robert and Lynsey. The Barton family along with the Waites—Wilber, Nancy, and their five kids—had gathered for an outdoor barbeque picnic to view the total solar eclipse that had been predicted for many months. According to news reports, the sun would be completely blotted out by the moon as viewed from this part of Iowa at around five o'clock in the afternoon on August 7. Everyone was excited about the rare chance to see a total eclipse of the sun. Bill surveyed the growing herd of Waite and Barton kids as they played on blankets spread out on the grass to await the magic hour. Children were the future and he knew he would never tire of watching them grow. With new land opening in the west, the country would need young men and women to tame it. He was proud that his children would be among them.

Bill regretted that Lucy and he had never been officially married, but he hoped that one day he would buy her a diamond ring and give her the church wedding he had promised her. He knew however they would never be able to lead a normal life until Cole Younger and his brothers were captured or killed. He could never take his guard down as long as the desperadoes roamed free. He was convinced that Cole would never give up searching for them.

Bill was unable to forget the words Cole had engraved into the band of the diamond wedding ring he had planned to give to Lucy: "Two Hearts Beating as One." The way Cole had spoken those words out loud with a shaking voice for the first time that day in the jewelry store had told Bill that the man truly loved Lucy Breeden with all his heart. The realization that Cole loved Lucy had amazed Bill more than anything. Cole's secret sentiment had captured exactly how Bill himself felt about Lucy. If the situation was reversed, if he was Cole, he knew he wouldn't rest until he tracked down and killed the dirty scoundrel who stole the love of his life before he took her back for himself. He also knew nothing would be able to hold him back from carrying out that single-minded mission. It was that chilling thought that kept Bill ever vigilant and had made him a man who could find little rest.

With these foreboding thoughts swirling around in his mind, he joined the gathering. Wilber, who had been studying how to make a pin-hole camera to monitor the progress of the eclipse, was busy trying to set up his makeshift contraption. He claimed that everyone would be able to safely watch the moon slowly cover the disc of the sun by watching the circle of sunlight shining on a piece of white cloth he had situated under the tiny hole he had drilled into a board propped up on two chairs. Bill had his doubts and saw that Lucy and Nancy were just as skeptical.

It wasn't long, however, until several of Wilber's older kids began screeching with excitement as the circle of sunlight became a crescent which grew thinner and thinner as the moon slowly covered the sun. Strangely, the air became cooler as the light of the sun noticeably dimmed.

Then as if God himself had snubbed out the candle of the sun, they found themselves in the umbra and above them, where once the sun had shined brightly, appeared a black hole in the heavens surrounded by milky coronal light radiating out into the darkened heavens. The mystical beauty of the spectacle left everyone in awe. Each knew no words could ever express the wonder of the mystery unfolding before them.

Everything seemed to stop. Birds, animals, and even insects seemed to fall silent. The chickens roosted as if evening had fallen. The air grew increasing cooler. Everyone stared into the black hole of the sun as though they were looking into infinity itself. As quickly as it had come, the spell was broken when the first rays of the sun burst free, creating a perfect diamond ring effect. Though the illusion was over in an instant, its memory would last a lifetime.

With the sun once again burning brightly, everyone was abuzz talking about their collective experience. Bill couldn't shake the ominous feeling the diamond ring effect had left with him.

"Bill, did you see it?" Lucy said with excitement in her voice. "It was amazing, a perfect diamond ring. Its stone a burst of sunrays shooting out in every direction." Lucy's eyes were still wide with wonder as she tried to fully comprehend what they had just witnessed.

"Yes, it was unbelievable. I've never seen anything so wonderous," Bill agreed. Bill too was left with a vision of wonder he knew he would never forget.

"Seeing that diamond ring reminded me of the ring you told me Cole bought for me in Kansas City," Lucy said in a voice nearly a whisper. "The one that tipped you off about his early wedding plans. It sent a chill down my spine, Bill. Do you think he'll ever find us?" Lucy continued, her eyes suddenly full of concern.

"Oh Lucy, I'd bet ya he's sold that ol' ring a long time ago," Bill said, trying to comfort her. "We'll always keep an eye out for him as long as he's on the loose," Bill added. "These days, however, I think the James-Younger Gang has a damn sight more to worry about than beatin' the bushes for Cole Younger's long-lost sweetheart."

"I pray you are right. Don't forget what Pappy said in his last letter. Cole's been visitin' him on a regular basis for over two years now," Lucy reminded Bill. "You know, he hasn't given up."

After settling into Lizard Creek, Lucy had discovered Nancy had a cousin who lived down in northwestern Missouri not far from the Little

Platte. Nancy's cousin soon became a reliable conduit for safely passing messages between Lucy and Pappy.

"I read Pappy's letter," Bill said, feeling a little stung by her reminder. "I just think Cole's rise to fame has made it less likely he has the time to chase after us," he continued, still trying to dispel Lucy's concern.

"Bill Barton, you don't believe that and you sure as hell don't have to coddle me," Lucy fired back, her eyes narrowing, her temper flaring. "You know damn well he'd gun you down like a dog on sight and take me without a thought about what might happen to our kids."

"Whoa, I know you know, and I understand Pappy's concerns. I just don't want you worryin' so much all the time," Bill said, keeping his voice low, not wanting to create a scene. He had been at the wrong end of Lucy's temper more than once, and since Alda's birth, her fuse had become a damn sight shorter. He understood a woman's emotions were sometimes a bit raw right after childbirth. He also had to admit she was right to worry about Cole and deserved to know the truth about his own concerns.

"I'm worried too, but I think we are safe here," Bill continued. "Being near Fort Dodge with its full garrison of troops is also in our favor. If the James-Younger Gang ever comes up Iowa way, you can be sure they'll steer clear of this part of the state."

"I just don't like being treated like a child or being lied to," Lucy said, her temper cooling as quickly as it had flared. "I know you mean well, and I love you, Bill, but you have to be straight with me," she added, the look on her face deadly serious.

Bill nodded and gave Lucy a hug as little Alda squirmed in her arms. Lucy's words had hit him hard. He knew there was much he hadn't shared with her about his days as Leroy Thompson or about his real fears of Cole Younger finding their hideaway on Lizard Creek. He knew he would have to tell her about his life as an outlaw one day, when the time was right. He wondered when that might be.

When Bill witnessed the diamond ring effect, he too had thoughts of Cole Younger and his diamond ring for Lucy. He too had experienced a cold chill run down his spine. His instincts told him the vision was an omen. He wasn't sure at the time whether it was an ill omen, one of past sins and retribution due; or a good omen, one of good fortune and happier days ahead. He knew if it was an omen, other signs would help reveal its deeper meaning. He feared however that it seemed more likely an ill omen, considering it had triggered the same visceral reaction and same raw memories of Cole Younger and his wedding plans in them both.

Seeking a further sign that might point to an answer, Bill only found a cloudless sky and the high-pitched shrill of a male katydid relentlessly calling out to his long-lost mate ringing in his ears. Bill had little doubt as to the meaning of the sign. Cole Younger, like the relentless katydid, would never give up searching for his long-lost mate, Lucy Breeden.

June 03, 1871

Louisville, Jefferson County, Kentucky

Loose Ends

Though it seemed like yesterday, years had passed since Bill had been in Louisville, Kentucky. Like other border states during the war, Kentucky had been proslavery and anti-secession. During the war, Louisville had been a major Union Army stronghold where Bill had often visited to pass on intelligence before returning to the South. He had always enjoyed spending time in the lively city during the war. He now found himself spooked and constantly looking over his shoulder every time he turned the next corner. He had felt uneasy since boarding the train to St. Louis to catch the steamboat that brought him to Louisville less than two days ago. He wasn't sure what was making him feel so jumpy, but he knew something wasn't right. His years working undercover told him he was being tracked.

Though he had reassured Lucy his quick business trip to Louisville would be safe since he would be steering clear of the Youngers' well-known haunts, he no longer felt so certain. Traveling anywhere in the South or even the border states where he could be identified as Leroy Thompson remained risky. He should have realized how raw the emotions remained in former Confederate territory since the war. He had run into many former rebels on the trip who made it clear they hadn't completely accepted the outcome of the war. The sooner he collected the money he was owed for the two thoroughbreds he had sold at auction that morning, the sooner he would be able to put Louisville and former rebel territory behind him. His scheduled meeting with the buyers was at the auction house at three o'clock, giving him plenty of time to catch the five o'clock steamboat bound for St. Louis. He had already bought his ticket and couldn't wait to be underway.

Thoroughbreds had become popular, being the perfect breed for flat racing. With the sport's popularity on the rise, prices for Arabian thoroughbreds had increased year on year. Bill had stolen three Arabian thoroughbreds, a stallion and two mares, from a burnt-out dilapidated plantation in northern Mississippi during his outlaw days just after the war and was pleased their foals were in demand. He figured the market for thoroughbreds would only get better in coming years, having learned that Colonel Meriwether Lewis Clark Jr., grandson of William Clark of the Lewis and Clark Expedition, was planning to travel to England sometime in the next year to study how professional thoroughbred racing might be established in Louisville. Little did anyone know at the time, the first Kentucky Derby featuring thoroughbreds would be run just four years later at a newly developed racetrack called Churchill Downs in Louisville, Kentucky on May 17, 1875.

Bill's thoughts of getting paid and getting out of town were unexpectedly interrupted by the sight of a tall well-dressed middle-aged man waving his arms and looking at him from the other side of the street.

"Leroy, Leroy, Leroy Thompson!" the man shouted as he made his way across the street, dodging horse-drawn buggies coming from both directions.

Bill couldn't believe his eyes. The man coming straight at him was Jacob O'Leary, a well-known rebel gunrunner and a man Bill had befriended to gain vital intelligence about Confederate battle plans and troop movements during the war, a man whose confidence he had betrayed on more than a few occasions.

"Jacob, that you?" Bill yelled back.

Making it across the busy street without incident, Jacob gripped Bill's extended right hand and gave it a hearty shake.

"It's been nearly seven years since I last saw you," Jacob said. "How the hell have you been since the war?"

"I've been doing fine, ever since I put the war behind me," Bill said, wondering what might be on Jacob's mind and hoping he too had put the war behind him.

Bill recalled that the last time he met Jacob, the man had told him that there were folks who suspected Leroy of working for the other side and had warned him to watch his back. Bill knew at the time that the folks who suspected Leroy were none other than Jacob himself.

"How about a drink for old time's sake? Be great to catch up," Jacob offered. "There's a great saloon just up the street called Bixby's," he coaxed, extending his arm with an open hand to show the way.

Bill knew he had no option but to accept Jacob's gracious offer. Everything about the sudden encounter, however, had put Bill on the alert for trouble. He feared Jacob was holding a grudge, considering how the war had turned out. Jacob wouldn't be the first man seeking to even the score after the war; Bill's personal experience confirmed that truth.

Jacob led the way to a dimly lit saloon on 3rd Street just off Broadway. Entering through the bat-winged doors, Jacob motioned for Bill to take a seat at a table in the middle of the room. Jacob stepped up to the bar and ordered a bottle of bourbon, a bottle of branch water, and a bucket of ice. Leaning over the bar, he had a few private words with the bartender, followed by a shared chuckle. Standing as if to block Bill's view, Jacob quickly wrote something on a small piece of paper he then slipped into his shirt pocket. His business at the bar complete, he yelled over to a barmaid to hurry up with his order before he joined Bill at the table.

A smiling barmaid showing plenty of cleavage soon brought Jacob's order on a large tray which she left in the middle of the table. Jacob tipped her with a silver dollar and slapped her on her bottom before she got out of reach. Looking back over her shoulder, she smiled and giggled at Jacob as she slowly and sensuously tucked the silver dollar down between her generous beasts with the tip of her index finger. Jacob smiled back, clearly enjoying her suggestive flirt.

"Girl's great in the sack," Jacob said with a crooked smile and wink. "The bartender has rooms upstairs beyond that green curtain. When I'm in town, I like coming here for a little fun from time to time," he added, motioning to the dark green curtain covering a hidden hallway leading to the back of the saloon.

Bill noted there were enough glasses on the tray for a party of three. Without comment, he sat tight, not much liking the direction things were going. It was no surprise Jacob, a southerner, had ordered a bucket of chiseled ice. Bill never forgot the ice famine he had experienced in the South during his years as a Union spy. Starved of New England ice imports, the South suffered a severe ice shortage throughout the war. He was sure Jacob also remembered those tough times and was still trying to make up for them.

The ice trade had expanded rapidly in the 1860s, especially after the end of the Civil War, bringing an end to the ice famine in the South.

Chilling food and beverages with ice soon became commonplace. By the 1870s the ice trade had become global in scope, with key suppliers like Norway, Alaska, Hudson Bay, and New England harvesting ice from freshwater lakes, streams, mill ponds, and fjords for markets around the world while Switzerland harvested ice from its Grindelwald glaciers for the European market.

"I like bourbon with a little branch water on the rocks. Helps to clean the palate," Jacob said with a chuckle. When their eyes met, Bill noted unlike Jacob's smiling face and friendly manner, his eyes held no laughter. Jacob made each of them a drink and offered up his glass in a toast.

"To better times, my friend," he said.

"Cheers to that," Bill replied as they clinked their glasses together over the table.

In the beginning, their conversation stayed light, with Jacob recounting how he had ended up in the cotton trade and often visited Louisville on business, and with Bill spinning a fresh tale about how he was in the cattle business and happened to be passing through Louisville on his way back east for business meetings.

It wasn't long before Jacob recounted how he had lost everything after the war. With the sudden defeat of the Confederacy, the tens of thousands of dollars in greybacks he had profiteered during the war had turned into worthless paper overnight, the money having been issued with only the promise to pay the bearer its face value upon the glorious victory of the Confederate States of America. The Confederacy's fiat currency had been printed and issued in the millions of dollars to fund the war without the backing of solid assets like silver or gold. When the war ended, greybacks were worth no more than the paper they were printed on.

"I was a true believer in the Confederate cause, my friend, but I was a goddamn fool not to demand Yankee greenbacks for every goddamn bullet I sold 'em," he concluded bitterly.

"We'd all believed," Bill said, wanting nothing more than to part company with Jacob before things got ugly.

"Did we? Did you?" he snapped. "I thought a guy like you might've made out just fine, seein' how you'd worked both sides during the war, Leroy," he continued, meeting Bill eye to eye.

"You know better. Just like you, I lost everything and everyone I ever loved in the war. I ended up no better off than you, Jacob," Bill said flatly.

"Well, Leroy, even if that were so, I heard you've been doin' pretty damn well with all your cattle rustlin' and outlawin' since the war. Hell, I even heard tell you stole Cole Younger's sweetheart," Jacob said as he topped off their glasses with bourbon. "Seems you like to steal things from other men. Their trust, their money, their horses, their cattle, their women," he added dryly, looking at Bill straight in the eye.

"You hear a lot, Jacob. Hear anything else?" Bill said, keeping his voice as calm as possible and wondering exactly what Jacob may have up his sleeve.

"Not much else. However, I did run into Cole Younger earlier today," Jacob said, acting nonchalant as he studied Bill's reaction to the news.

"So, Cole's in town, is he?" Bill said, his face an expressionless mask, his mind now racing a mile a minute in a frantic search for viable options.

"Yes, as a matter of fact he is. Says he'd like to meet ya. Seems he's never had the pleasure of meetin' ya face to face," Jacob said, with the grin on his face growing wider with each new revelation.

Just as Bill was ready to reply, a young boy in patched overalls stepped up to the table. "You need me to do somethin' for ya, mister? Mr. Mondale, the bartender there, says ya have somethin' for me," the boy said as he shuffled his feet and looked expectantly at Jacob.

Bill watched as Jacob and the bartender gave each other a knowing nod. "Yeah that's right, take this over to the New Mount Hotel, the man over there'll take care of ya," Jacob said as he passed a folded piece of paper to the boy. With that, the boy took off on the run.

"You know, you're right, Jacob. I don't believe Cole and I have ever had the pleasure," Bill said, finishing up his drink. "Maybe you can set somethin' up next time I'm in town. It's been a pleasure catchin' up and much obliged for the drinks," Bill added as he started to get up. Bill figured the boy had been given a note intended for Cole Younger who was probably waiting somewhere nearby, and he knew he had no time to waste.

Motioning for Bill to stay seated, Jacob quickly added, "No need to hurry off, Leroy, Cole'll be here soon. I asked'm to drop in. I told'm you'd be here. Said you'd be dying to meet'm."

Bill eased himself back down into his seat just as Jacob moved to pull a pistol on him under the table. "I wouldn't try that," Bill said flatly as he tapped the bottom of the table with the barrel of his own pistol, stopping Jacob in midmotion. Their movements frozen, the two men stared at each other as the hustle and bustle of the busy saloon continued to swirl around them. Bill could clearly see hatred etched into every line on Jacob's face. There was no doubt Jacob knew Leroy had betrayed him during the war and now wanted revenge. Bill figured Jacob had somehow learned Cole Younger was also looking for Leroy Thompson and had decided to use Cole's vengeance to settle his own score.

"Now, get up slow and easy and start walking toward that green curtain at the back of the room," Bill said as he motioned with his chin in the direction of the curtain.

Jacob slowly eased out of his chair and walked toward the curtain with Bill following close behind. Bill had holstered his pistol before he got up and casually rested the palm of his right hand on its butt. Going through the slit in the curtain, Bill looked back and saw both the bartender and buxom barmaid frantically talking to each other and giving him a suspicious look. Bill smiled, winked, and doffed his hat at them as he passed through the curtain, earning a loud chuckle and hearty giggle in reply. Passing through the curtain the sounds of the saloon nearly disappeared as the two men entered a dark narrow hallway. Halfway down the hallway, an arched opening on the left side of the hall was lit up from light spilling down a stairway that led upstairs, probably to where Jacob liked to have a little fun from time to time, Bill thought. As they approached the end of the hallway, Bill could see the silhouette of a door lit up by sunlight streaming in around its edges standing at the far end of what appeared to be a large storage room.

"Stop right here," Bill said.

Pressing his pistol barrel hard into Jacob's back, Bill slipped Jacob's pistol out of its holster and tucked it into his own gun belt. Jacob had become a dangerous loose end that would need to be deal with. As Bill weighed his options, Jacob made his move. Turning quickly, Jacob grabbed Bill's pistol hand and slammed it into the wall of the narrow hallway, sending Bill's pistol flying as Jacob brought up a knee into Bill's stomach, knocking the air out of him. Bill, gasping for air, lunged in desperation for Jacob's waist, sending both men to the floor. Still gasping for breath, Bill attempted to pin the man to the floor as he reached for the pistol he had just tucked into his gun belt. Jacob, countering Bill's clumsy moves, slammed his gun hand against the wall again sending the second pistol flying. Breaking free of Bill's grasp, Jacob rolled head over heels into the storage room, pulling a wicked-looking knife out of a sheath in his right boot. Bill had no more than regained his feet when Jacob came at him, slashing the knife's razor-sharp blade in broad arcs. Bill felt the blade slice across the front of his shirt, cutting through the material like a hot knife through butter.

Enraged, Jacob came at him again, flailing the knife like a mad man. Having nothing to block the razor-sharp blade and with no other options,

Bill took off his hat and held it in front of himself like a shield just as Jacob slashed down with his knife. As the knife sliced through the top of the hat, Bill stepped forward to parry the blow, inadvertently pulling the rim of the hat up Jacob's arm as the blade passed through. Surprised that he had somehow lassoed Jacob's arm, Bill quickly twisted the hat rim around Jacob's forearm, gaining a degree of control over the slashing blade. Using his tenuous hold on Jacob's arm, Bill drove the man backwards and then quickly dropped down and kicked his feet out from under him. Jacob came down hard on his back. Without missing a beat, Bill used his hat rim hold to twist the blade of the knife toward the fallen man's chest and then rammed it home by slamming the palm of his free hand into the butt of the knife. Stunned and surprised, Jacob looked up at Bill through tear-filled eyes, wishing in that fleeting moment he too had put the war behind him long ago. Holding his hand over Jacob's mouth to prevent any last second cries for help, Bill took no pleasure in shoving the blade deeper into Jacob's chest until he finally extinguished the last spark of life animating the hatred that had possessed the man.

Wasting no time, Bill quickly surveyed the room. After gathering up the two pistols, Bill put on Jacob's hat and tucked Jacob's sheathed knife into the shaft of his own right boot. Finding an empty pickle barrel behind a pile of stacked up boxes, Bill wedged Jacob's body into the barrel and sealed up the lid. After straightening everything up and double-checking for any signs of blood, he took a final look around before he slipped out of the back door and into the alley. He was sure they wouldn't find ol' Jacob anytime soon. At least not until he started to stink the place up. His bigger concern was getting out of town before he ran into Cole Younger. He knew if that happened, he would be the one to get pickled.

Cole had been relentless in his search for Leroy Thompson, since the man had run off with the love of his life, Lucy Breeden. He had asked everyone he met whether they knew Leroy Thompson or knew where he might be found. As the years passed, Cole became increasingly frustrated. He couldn't believe how many people had heard of Leroy Thompson and yet had no idea what the man looked like or where he came from. Cole had come to accept that Leroy, a loner without friends, had kept a damn low profile and had left few lasting impressions. Looking for Leroy was like chasing a ghost. Charlie Pitts and the James brothers claimed they would be able to identify Leroy on sight. As it turned out, they were among the rare few who said they could.

It was for this reason that Cole had become hopeful after a chance meeting with Jacob O'Leary, a rebel gunrunner who had supplied Quantrill's Raiders during the war. The chance meeting happened when Jacob was boarding the steamboat, the *Water Queen*, in St. Louis just as Cole was getting off, having just arrived back from a trip to New Orleans. Since Jacob had a couple of hours before the steamboat would cast off again, the two men had decided to have a drink and catch up on ol' times. During their conversation, Cole learned that Jacob had known Leroy Thompson during the war. He also learned that Jacob had his own axe to grind with Leroy. According to Jacob, Leroy had been double-dealing during the war and had probably been a Union spy. As it turned out, Jacob had caught a chance sighting of Leroy boarding a train bound for St. Louis and decided to track the man down. Unable to ride the same train, he had followed on a later train and made it to St. Louis only to find out Leroy had already boarded a steamboat bound for Louisville. He had waited overnight for the next steamboat to Louisville in hopes of catching up with the son-of-a-bitch. Since he knew Louisville well, he figured he would have no trouble finding Leroy once he got there.

Hearing Jacob's tale and learning Leroy might have been a Union spy convinced Cole that he now knew why Leroy had been so damn tough to track down. He couldn't believe his good fortune in having run into Jacob. Cole told Jacob how Leroy had kidnapped Lucy and how he had been searching for Leroy for four years without much luck. Jacob assured Cole he could identify Leroy Thompson on sight and offered to team up with Cole to track the man down. Rather than getting off the *Water Queen* in St. Louis, Cole paid the extra fare and joined Jacob on his journey up the Ohio River to Louisville.

After landing in Louisville, Cole wasted no time in buying a horse and getting it outfitted. Jacob told Cole he would be sending a messenger to the New Mount Hotel on 7th Street by noon and to be ready. Jacob made it clear that he had become well-known in Louisville and needed to protect his reputation. Though he would be happy to point out the target, Cole would have to do the shooting. Cole had to chuckle at the thought of a man who needed others to do his dirty work for him. Cole had never minded getting his hands dirty. Fact was, he liked to get 'em dirty and when it came to Leroy Thompson, he relished the thought.

Cole was seated in a large hickory rocker on the front porch of the hotel having a smoke, when a young boy ran up to him holding a folded piece of paper. Cole took the folded paper and flipped the boy a fifty-cent piece for his trouble. Opening the note, the scrawled handwritten message was clear enough,

Hurry, Bixby's on 3rd Street just off Broadway—He's here

For the first time in a long time, Cole felt a little giddy. The prey he had hunted for so many years was finally in his sights. As much as he wanted to killed Leroy Thompson, he needed to keep him alive long enough to find his Lucy-belle Breeden. Touching the diamond ring hanging near his heart, he was certain Lucy-belle would be his once again, and very soon. He checked his pistol load and slid a cartridge into the blank cylinder under the pistol's hammer. The extra precaution of leaving an empty cylinder under the hammer was only a disadvantage for a man headed to a gunfight.

Cole barged through the bat-winged doors and into the dimly lit saloon with his head swiveling and his right hand hovering over his holstered pistol. He quickly surveyed the room as a hush came over the customers who sat looking at Cole wondering who he might be looking for. A busty barmaid cleaning off a table in the center of the room stood wide-eyed with a look of confusion on her face.

"Leroy, you in here?" Cole barked, wondering why Jacob was nowhere in sight.

The room remained silent until a rough-looking character leaning on the bar with a drink in his hand said, "Who the hell wants to know?"

"Leroy, that you?" Cole questioned, not really believing he had finally tracked down the son-of-bitch, Leroy Thompson. He also wondered how Lucy-belle could have ever run off with such a sorry-looking bastard.

"Where's my woman?" Cole demanded. "If ya tell me now and tell me the truth, I just might let ya live."

"Your woman? Was that little bitch your woman?" the man tauntingly laughed. "Damn man, I dumped her off at the first whorehouse I could find. They didn't pay me much for her scrawny ass, but I'd be happy to buy you a drink," he said as he finished the drink in his hand and carefully placed the glass on the counter, freeing his right hand.

"You sold my Lucy-belle to a whorehouse? What the hell's wrong with ya, man?" Cole stammered in disbelief. Cole stood momentarily disarmed as his mind swam with horrifying thoughts of his Lucy-belle now lost to him forever.

"Lucy-belle? Is that what you called the little whore? She called herself Rose. She was a pretty little thing, but she had plenty of thorns," the man said with a grin on his face. "Now, who the hell are you?" the man questioned, pushing his duster back to free his pistol.

"Rose? Her name was Lucy. Why would she call herself Rose?" Cole said, confused.

"Hell man, I have no idea. She wanted to run off with somebody, so I obliged," he said flatly. "She was a good ride. Can't say it wasn't fun while it lasted," he added with a chuckle.

"So, you're sayin' Lucy called herself Rose?" Cole said, starting to wonder what was really going on.

"Guess so," the man said, playing with Cole.

"I'm looking for Lucy Breeden. She was my woman and I want her back," Cole said through clenched teeth, his temper on the verge of exploding.

"Look buckaroo, she was goin' to run off, with or without my help. Can't blame a man for helping himself to a little tail when it's offered," the man said as he looked around the saloon, satisfied with the size of the crowd and that he now had everyone's attention.

"She wouldn't have run off without you takin' her," Cole challenged.

"You callin' me a liar?" the man asked.

"Yep, that's right. I'm calling you a goddamn liar," Cole growled.

The man's draw was a blur, much faster than Cole expected; unable to take a chance on anything but a head shot, Cole's first shot hit the man squarely in his left eye, blowing out a large chunk of the left side of his head. With his sudden loss of motor control, the man's pistol flew out of his limp hand, firing harmlessly into the floor. For good measure, Cole pumped a second and a third round into the man's chest, causing his body to tip over backwards and fall as stiff as a cigar store Indian.

Cole stood stock-still and stared at the man's lifeless body as everyone in the saloon froze, uncertain of what might come next. Gun smoke drifted in the air, the only sound in the saloon coming from the busy street beyond the bat-winged doors. Cole couldn't believe what he had heard and felt broken-hearted to have learned that Lucy, if she was still alive, was now no more than a common whore. He retched at the thought of what if anything might be left of her innocence and beauty after all these years.

"Jumpin' Jehoshaphat mister, you just gunned down Dan Bogan!" the bartender blurted with a shocked look on his face. "He was one of the fastest guns there ever was," he continued, his last words spoken in awe.

"Dan Bogan? So, you're sayin' that's not Leroy Thompson laying there?" Cole said, confused, looking at the bartender for answers.

"No mister, I know, well, I knew Dan Bogan. No mistake, that's Dan Bogan layin' there," the bartender stammered matter-of-factly.

"Why the hell did he answer to Leroy then?" Cole asked, still confused.

"He liked to put himself into the middle of other folk's troubles. He got a kick out of it," the bartender replied, still in shock about what he had just witnessed.

"Well, I guess he got a bigger kick than he bargained for this time," Cole said dryly. "Now, where the hell is Leroy Thompson? And has anyone seen Jacob O'Leary?" he barked as he looked around the room while reloading his pistol.

The room remained silent until the bartender spoke once again. "O'Leary was just here with another fella I'd never seen before. I saw 'em head upstairs just before you got here," the bartender said, motioning to the green curtain in the back of the room.

Like a man possessed, Cole ran through the curtain, down the narrow hallway, and up the stairway only to find two tired-looking whores and a couple of Louisville's finest upstanding citizens all dressed in varying degrees of meager attire. After a search of the premises, neither Jacob nor Leroy were anywhere to be found. With the law on the way, Cole reluctantly gave up the search and decided to put Louisville behind him. Having learned about Leroy's activities during the war and where he might find others able to identify him, Cole felt his encounter with Jacob O'Leary hadn't been a complete bust. He wondered what might have happened to Jacob, but somehow knew he would never see the man again. Considering Leroy had been able to give Cole the slip just in the nick of time, Cole was sure Leroy had somehow been able to permanently tie off the O'Leary loose end before making his escape. Cole had to admit he had underestimated Leroy Thompson and wouldn't make the same mistake again.

After his bizarre encounter with Dan Bogan and hearing his horrible make-believe story about Lucy, Cole felt strangely relieved to know his Lucy-belle was still with Leroy Thompson and still safe. Touching the diamond ring hanging next to his heart, he knew that one day Lucy-belle would wear the ring and share the engraved sentiment etched into its band with the man whose heart beat as one with hers. He believed he was that man. With renewed hope, Cole returned to the hotel, mounted his horse, and headed southeast away from the Ohio River straight into Kentucky hill country. In coming days, he would work his way west to Paducah on the Ohio River to catch a steamboat to St. Louis and home.

Bill had escaped Bixby's only moments before Cole had busted through its bat-winged doors. That Dan Bogan, a well-known gunslinger and trickster, had been in the saloon, had baited Cole into a gunfight by pretending to be Leroy Thompson, and had ended up dead were details Bill would only learn secondhand, years after the events. All Bill was able to recount about what happened in Louisville when he got back to Lizard Creek was that when Jacob O'Leary had told him Cole Younger was in town and on his way, he had run like hell out of the saloon and ended up hiding out in the auction house until his buyers settled their bill. In coming years, whenever Bill was asked about what happened to Jacob O'Leary, he would only say Jacob had been a man who had been unable put the war behind him. Bill often added, a lesson about life he had learned from his father long ago, "A man who dwells in the past not only deprives himself of the present, but robs himself of the future."

When Bill finally boarded his scheduled steamboat, the *Cairo Star*, he promised himself he would be staying closer to home until Cole Younger was no longer on the loose. He knew his hat rim lasso and narrow escape had been nothing but a fluke. He also knew Jacob O'Leary hadn't been the only loose end from his past that might still be out there. Though Cole Younger was Bill's biggest threat, he wasn't the only man in the South who would like to even the score with Leroy Thompson.

Bill was shaken by the events in Louisville and by just how close he had come to losing everything. Standing on deck, he searched for any sign that might help guide his and Lucy's way through an uncertain future. The river ran low, causing the heavily laden steamboat to frequently scrape on sandbars as it slowly weaved its way downriver while keeping to the river's deeper channels. Bill watched the pilot up in the wheelhouse as he nimbly steered the clumsy craft. Though he allowed the bottom of the boat to scrap a few shallow sandbars, he adroitly avoided the bigger snags while maintaining a steady speed forward. Bill took this as the sign he was looking for; he too would need to steer a steady course while avoiding the bigger snags as he and Lucy moved cautiously down their river of life together. Staying in deeper water and away from the shallows was good advice if you wanted to avoid predators prowling on the shoreline. Bill only hoped that the information Jacob had given Cole about Leroy Thompson and his activities during the war wouldn't stir up any predators that might be slumbering in deeper waters as well.

March 22, 1874

Boonville, Cooper County, Missouri

Code of the Outlaw

COLE PUT DOWN HIS drink and leaned back from the bar to peer out through grease-smudged windows for a better view of all the commotion coming from the front of the saloon. The sounds of men dismounting their horses, the jingling of tac and spurs, and the popping sounds of men brushing trail dust off their clothes filled the silence of the near-empty saloon. As soon as the three riders bucked through the bat-winged doors, Cole's expression turned from a squint-eyed scowl to a wide-eyed grin. As he eased his hand off the butt of his pistol, he moved forward to welcome the new arrivals.

"Good to see you boys could make it to the party," Cole said with a grin.

Frank James and Jim and Bob Younger strolled into the saloon and took a table on the back wall facing the front. All three men grabbed a chair and gestured for Cole to join them.

"Well, we're here. Now where the hell is that dancing bear you promised us, Cole?" Frank said as he looked around the empty room, as if he were expecting to find the long-lost bear hiding in one of the corners or under a table somewhere.

"Why hell Franky, you know'd we ate the son-of-a-bitch a long time ago," Cole said flatly, the remark causing a spasm of laugher to infect the whole gang.

"Bartender, bring us a bottle of whiskey and glasses," Cole barked. "We have some serious drinkin' to do." The boys all laughed while filling their glasses, waiting to talk until after the bartender returned to his station behind the bar.

"Now boys, where the hell are Jesse and little Johnny?" Cole said in a low voice.

"Well, I hate to be to one to break the bad news, Cole, but Johnny was kilt three days ago in a shootout near Roscoe, in Saint Clair County," Jim said, his voice cracking when he uttered the word *kilt*. "I was with him when we got jumped by Pinkerton agents. We kilt one of the Pinky bastards and a deputy out a St. Clair County named Ed Daniels. After Johnny went down, I barely got out of there alive," Jim continued with tears in his eyes, clearly shaken. Jim couldn't shake off the experience of having his little brother die in his arms. Even though he knew there had been no way to save his little brother's life, he felt responsible. The incident would remain an emotional scar that would haunt Jim Younger for the rest of his life.

"Damn, those rotten Pinkerton scum," Cole said, shaking his head and trying to keep his emotions under control. "They've been tracking us for months. We're goin' to have to kill every one of the bastards we can find to chase 'em out of Missouri. The time's come to gun down the tricky devils on sight. No amount of blood'll ever bring Johnny back, but I'll not rest until I spill a hell of a lot more of theirs. How did mama take the news?" Cole continued, clearly in shock and angered over the sudden news of his little brother's death. Unlike Cole and Jim who had fought in the war, their younger brothers Bob and John had stayed home with their mother to tend to the family farm. Losing little Johnny, his baby brother, left a hole in Cole he wasn't sure would ever heal.

Rattled by Johnny's untimely and violent death, Cole's mind wandered into a grove of long suppressed thoughts, thoughts he had harbored since Leroy Thompson stole his lovely Lucy-belle, thoughts he had not taken time to mull over for some time, thoughts of finding Lucy-belle and taking her back, thoughts of giving up his outlaw ways and never looking back, thoughts of walking hand and hand with the beautiful Lucy-belle Breeden on a sandy beach along the Pacific coast, thoughts of living a life free of violence and the gun.

"Mama took it hard. She said we should make 'em pay for what they did, first to pa and now to little Johnny. She said it was time for some payback," Jim said, hitting the table hard with his balled-up fists, causing glasses to jump and whiskey to splash across the table.

Cole jumped at the sound of his brother's fists banging on the table, which caused his wandering mind to crash back into the harsh reality that faced him and the rest of the gang. With his mind still swimming, he had the unshakable certainty that the course of his life had somehow changed forever.

Though his father, Henry Washington Younger, had initially supported the Union cause, his death by a Union soldier had changed Cole and driven him and his brothers to seek revenge by joining the Confederate cause and ultimately Quantrill's Raiders. Now the sudden and violent death of his youngest brother Johnny by Pinkerton scum had driven Cole once again to seek a change in his life, a change he hoped would end his life's current reckless course and reunite him with the love of his life, Lucy-belle Breeden.

"There'll be time for mourning the dead after the job," Cole said, rubbing his temples to collect his wits while trying to charge ahead. "So now, who's riding with Jesse? And, where the hell are they?"

"Charlie Pitts and Clell Miller will join the party. They'll be ridin' in soon," Frank said, quickly wanting to get things back on track. "The new plan is for Jesse and Charlie to join you in the bank. They'll come in after you take a position near the tellers. Me, Clell, and the boys here will watch the street from each end of town and in front of the bank," Frank continued, knowing the plan had changed since the last time they had talked with Cole. Frank also knew last-minute changes never went down well with Cole.

"What the hell, this isn't what we talked about a couple weeks ago. Jesse and you, Frank, and I were to go into the bank together while the others all guarded the front and the street. Why the sudden changes?" Cole said, wanting to make it clear he was in charge.

"Jesse learned they have an armed guard in the bank, better to have a steady gun hand already in there to get the drop on him before Jesse and Charlie come busting in," Frank said in a calm voice, not wanting the matter to turn into a pissing contest.

"Jesse'd wanted Johnny to hold the horses but . . . he had to bring in Charlie and Clell and change a few things up," Frank continued, not sure how Cole would respond.

"Alright, alright, I can see why Jesse changed things up. Johnny gettin' kilt and an armed guard in the bank have changed things considerable. If the armed guard tries anything, we may have to kill'm," Cole said, his eyes burning with his growing need to avenge his little brother's untimely death. "Damn right, there's no tellin' just how messy things might get if folks start throwin' lead. They're probably all blue-bellies in this part of the state anyway. Hell, if a few catch some lead, no big loss either way."

"All well and good Cole, but Jesse would like to get in and out as quickly and as peaceable-like as possible. No gun-play. We'll gun 'em if we have to, but it's best to keep folks thinkin' kindly of us. Killin' town folk, even blue-bellies, tends to turn folks sour on us and what we're doing. Hell, Cole, we're like Robin Hood to these folks. No need in spoiling our good reputations," Frank said with a smirk on his face echoing Jesse's words, words everyone in the gang had heard Jesse repeat more and more often lately. There was no arguing that as the bodies piled up, resistance from law enforcement, Pinkertons, and local citizens had stiffened considerably. The big reason Jesse had turned to robbing trains and to avoiding robbing any of the passengers if possible was an attempt to reduce the body count which helped the gang stay on the good side of public opinion.

"Yeah, yeah, I've heard Jesse's constant preaching about not killin' town folk. But I've also seen him gun down some son-of-a-bitch at the drop of a hat that didn't pay him proper respect. Hell, he's shot folks he didn't like whether they were armed or not," Cole said, more than a little ticked off at having Frank lecture him on what Jesse might be wanting or not wanting. Jesse might be their undisputed leader, but this didn't make his brother Frank second in charge. Cole believed he held that position, considering that more than half the gang was made up of Youngers, and he didn't like having anyone, especially Frank James, challenge it.

"That may be, but that was then, and this is now," Frank said not backing down from Cole and meeting his glare eyeball to eyeball. Considering Cole's mood and his clear desire to draw blood over his youngest brother's untimely death, Frank now had his doubts about using Cole to cover the armed guard inside the bank.

Jim Younger, always the quiet one, seldom spoke up. When he did, it was usually for good reason. "Settle down, everyone," Jim said, cutting in with the aim of breaking the silent tension that was on the verge of exploding with the potential of violence between the two men. "How about another drink? Jesse, Charlie, and Clell should be here in an hour or so. After they get here, we can take our horses up the street a bit and then saunter on over near the bank," Jim continued, looking back and forth at Cole and Frank.

"Sounds like a plan, Jim," Frank said, still staring down Cole. "A hell of a plan. I sure hope Jesse doesn't show up too soon though. I'd like to polish off this here bottle of whiskey before he gets here," Frank added as he refilled Cole's glass and then his own, his stare never wavering. The two men continued to stare each other down until Frank lifted his glass and broke his stare, nodding to Cole in a sign of respect.

"Yes sir, it sounds like a mighty fine plan. Bottoms up boys!" Cole bellowed, and with that the tension flowed out of the outlaws as the whiskey burned all the way down, filling their guts with the courage they would need in the coming hours.

Three hard-looking men stepped into the saloon in late afternoon. Catching sight of the table on the back wall, Charlie Pitts and Clell Miller gathered up chairs from nearby tables while Jesse swung by the bar and grabbed three glasses and a bottle of whiskey before joining the rest of the gang.

Settling into the last open chair at the table, Jesse quickly got down to business. "Damn boys, ain't y'all a sight for sore eyes. We had a little lookin' around to do before ridin' into town," Jesse said as he took a shot of whiskey, wiping his lips with the back of his gloved hand.

"Lookin' around? What kind of lookin' around did you need to do? We already looked things over. We just need to hit the bank and ride like hell," Cole said, still stinging over his spat with Frank.

"Just needed to make sure when we ride out of here, we ride out in the right direction. The law is crawling all over this place and I don't need to remind anybody, Pinkerton agents could be anywhere. They wear disguises and pretend to be local town folk until they shoot you in the back. After what happened to Jim and Johnny, I thought we should be extra careful," Jesse said, fixing his stare on Cole.

"What'd ya find?" Cole said easing back in his chair and taking another drink.

"Best to ride south and then double back for five miles to that little shack just off Boone's Lick Trail. We can stop in there to split up the loot and then go our separate ways. We'll all meet up back in Jackson County once things settle down," Jesse said, making sure everyone understood the plan. The expressions on the grim faces he surveyed told him they all understood and were ready for action.

"Hey, Charlie. Hey, Clell. Good to have ya both join the party," Cole said as he held up his glass full of whiskey and lifted it up and down in a symbolic toast as he greeted each man. "You men look thirsty, you best fill up them glasses and catch up with the rest of this good-for-nothing bunch before they empty that second bottle," he continued, causing an eruption of good-natured laughter to ripple around the table.

Clell Miller was a short man with long red hair, ruddy skin, and a slender build with a permanent snarl on his face under a mangy unkept mustache. His eyes were like slits that held cold dark marbles of stone under a pinched brow. He wore a gentleman's derby, a tight black leather vest, and matching black leather holsters hung low and fastened to each leg with leather straps. His matching pearl-handled pistols were his calling cards. Clell Miller was a gunslinger. He had joined Quantrill's Raiders when he was only fourteen, and like Jesse James, he had ridden with Bloody-Bill Anderson. Toward the end of the war, he was captured by Union troops during the ambush that killed Bloody-Bill. Due to his youth he had been spared the hangman's noose. After only six months in captivity, he was released during the general amnesty after the end of war in April 1865. Soon after, he hooked up with his old comrade-in-arms, Jesse James, and returned to his outlaw ways.

Charlie Pitts was a regular with the gang. Cole and Jim Younger liked his quick wit and unwavering loyalty. Clell Miller joined the gang whenever Jesse thought they might need an additional gun hand. With the bank hiring an armed guard and increased Pinkerton activity in the area, Jesse wanted to take no chances on being outgunned.

Jesse watched as the gang swapped stories for nearly an hour as the whiskey flowed freely. Everyone had settled into a good mood. As if on cue, Jesse and Cole looked at each other and agreed with a nod; it was time. Frank, picking up on the silent communication, nodded to Jesse and Cole. They nodded back.

"One for the road then," Frank said, getting everyone's attention. He then held up his whiskey glass filled to the brim.

After everyone filled their glasses to the brim, they all stood up and clinked their glasses together over the middle of the table. In a ritual they had followed since becoming outlaws, they tipped up their glasses and drained them to the last drop and then clapped them down hard on the top of the table, bottoms up.

The next few minutes passed quickly as the men moved like clockwork. Before long Cole had entered the bank alone, with Jesse and Charlie not far behind. Time slowed as the men watching the street also readied the horses. Townsfolk ambled down the boardwalks without a care. No one seemed to notice the outsiders in their midst.

Shots rang out of the bank, sending the people on the streets ducking for cover. Jim, Bob, Clell, and Frank mounted their horses. Frank moved closer to the front of the bank while holding the reins of Jesse, Cole, and Charlie's horses. The outlaws now mounted and ready to ride watched both ways down the street, their guns drawn.

More shots followed as the three men ran out of the bank and quickly mounted their horses. Without missing a beat, the outlaws moving as one all spurred their horses, hightailing it out of town. A few random gunshots echoed behind them, but the bandits knew there weren't many men in these parts who could hit a moving target especially one getting smaller by the second. Just as they cleared the last outbuilding at the edge of town, rifle shots erupted from bushes on both sides of the trail.

Without missing a beat, Clell yelled out, "Tuck in behind me! We're charging through!"

Taking the lead, Clell quickly flipped his reins through loops hanging from conchos on both sides of his saddle's pommel and pulled out his pearl-handled pistols. Riding hands free at a full gallop, his red hair streaming out from under his Derby, he peppered the bushes on both sides of the trail with a hail of bullets as he blazed a trail for the gang riding behind him in tight formation. Jim and Charlie riding side by side just behind Clell also fired their pistols into the bushes on each side of the trail. Once the gang was in the clear, Jesse felt he had been vindicated in changing up the plan and in bringing in an extra gun hand. There was no doubt in Jesse's mind that Clell's quick actions had saved the gang's bacon.

None of the men tried to speak as they urged their horses to run like the wind. Frank was not sure what might have happened in the bank, but he was certain it was a vengeful Cole Younger who fired the first shot. He was also sure someone got themselves killed over someone else's money. A damn shame, but then Frank knew there were a lot of lost causes men chose to die for that they shouldn't have. More and more, he wondered if dying for a Confederacy that was already dead was something he really believed in any more. Frank knew these were dangerous thoughts, thoughts he wouldn't be sharing with anyone in the gang any time soon, especially with his brother Jesse.

They rode hard until they were able to travel up a small creek as they doubled back to catch the Boone's Lick Trail. Everyone began to focus on how much cash the two large bags of loot slung across Jesse's saddle horn might be holding. Jesse had been the first man out of the bank and was the one who had taken charge of the money.

Cole knew most of the men would head straight to St. Louis or even as far south as New Orleans, Texas, or even Mexico to get drunk, gamble, and chase whores. Cole, in a state of deep depression, couldn't stop thinking about how little Johnny had been hunted and gunned down like a dog by Pinkertons. Drawing blood in the bank had in no way evened the score. Cole was now more certain than ever that he wanted to escape his outlaw life and to settle down out west with the beautiful Lucy-belle Breeden, a dream he had secretly held in his heart for many years, a dream he now knew he could no longer suppress. As a reminder to himself of business yet undone, he patted the diamond wedding ring he had hung around his neck on a leather strap since that fateful day in Buchanan County when he discovered Lucy-belle had been abducted by a good-for-nothing horse thief named Leroy Thompson.

Though nearly seven years had passed, Cole hadn't given up hope. Over the years, he and his brothers had combed the countryside far and wide and had talked to many men who had known Leroy Thompson, only to come up empty. No one seemed to know where Leroy had come from or where he might have gone. Since Cole's chance meeting with Jacob O'Leary and his near miss in tracking down Leroy Thompson in Louisville, Cole had discovered there was a lot more to Leroy than his being a common horse thief. The additional information, however, changed nothing as far as Cole was concerned. He wanted his Lucy-belle back and was determined to find her. Cole knew that one day he would track down Leroy Thompson and kill the no-good son-of-a-bitch once and for all. He had made up his mind long ago that with Leroy out of the way, he would take back Lucy-belle for his bride and head straight to California, leaving his outlaw life behind forever.

To make this dream come true, he knew he would need plenty of money. Jesse had shared his plan to take down a fat Yankee bank up north with Cole some months ago. Once the gang took down the First National Bank up in Mankato, Minnesota, where Jesse was certain plenty of ill-gotten Reconstruction money was being squirreled away by a passel of mangy, low-down Yankee carpetbaggers, he would have all the money he and Lucy-belle would ever need. Cole now more than ever believed in Jesse's big plan. He was certain the money would be there. Cole couldn't help grinning as he daydreamed about being a free man way out west in California beyond the reach of the law with the love of his life, the beautiful Lucy-belle, on his arm and wads of cash in his pockets.

Once the men all gathered in the rickety shack off Boone's Lick Trail, it took no time to split up the loot. As it had been many times in the past, after the money had been divided into equal shares, there remained a single odd dollar.

"Cole, this time, you keep the last odd dollar, I'll keep the next one," Jesse said with a grin as he flipped the silver dollar to Cole and spurred his horse into a gallop.

Cole, still daydreaming, reached out half-heartedly for the coin, but missed catching it, the coin flying off into a dark corner of the shack. Cole being the last rider out, looked in the little shack for the coin, but couldn't see where the coin landed. Knowing every moment was precious and having over a thousand dollars in his saddlebags, Cole decided to leave the odd dollar behind. Taking one last look around, Cole mounted his horse and rode out.

By the time the posse reached the little shack off Boone's Lick Trail, rain showers had passed over, washing out the outlaws' tracks. From here on the trail had grown cold, the bandits long gone. With an armed guard and a bank teller killed in a hail of bullets and two bystanders critically wounded in the exchange of gunfire, not to mention three Pinkerton agents wounded in a botched ambush at the edge of town, word would spread far and wide of the brazen and ruthless acts of the James-Younger Gang. Support for their lawlessness had weakened, but not nearly enough, thought the sheriff. He knew the hunt for the James-Younger Gang wouldn't end here. The day would come, and soon, he felt deep down in his bones, when the James-Younger Gang would finally be tracked down and made to pay for their crimes.

"Sheriff, over here in the shack," one of his posse yelled, breaking into the sheriff's thoughts.

Sheriff Sam Jefferson had a face as weathered as a fence post, with deep grooves cut into its leather-tough skin. His eyes were like shards of green crystalline jade and peered through narrow slits under a furrowed brow. He sported a Van Dyke with a bushy handlebar mustache, just like Wild Bill Cody's, he liked to tell anyone who asked. His stride displayed all the years of a man nearing sixty who had lived a hard life, a life that had dealt him more than a few tough blows. Though he may have been wobbled a time or two in his life, his manner made it clear to everyone around him, he was still standing strong. When he arrived at the little shack, he found Pete Simpson pointing at an object oddly lodged into a crack between two boards near the back corner of the shack. The object had been lit up like a beacon by a shaft of sunlight coming in through a hole in the roof.

"Doesn't seem natural, that thing being all shiny and new in this old hut," Pete said, looking at the object more closely.

Seeing where Pete was pointing, Sam stepped into the little shack. "It's a shiny new Morgan silver dollar, minted just this year, 1874," the sheriff said as he pulled the coin out of a crack between two boards in the far corner of the shack and looked at the date.

"I'll be damned. Not sure why those hombres would leave a shiny new silver dollar behind. Damn strange. You think it's a calling card or some-thin'?" Pete said tipping his hat back to scratch his bald head.

"No Pete, it's a mistake. Simple as that," Sam said flatly. "Not sure what happened here, but we now know they came this way for sure. The bank pa-pers and bonds will be buried nearby here someplace. Tell the men to start lookin'. It seems the James-Younger Gang is gettin' sloppy in its old age," Sam added as he studied the shiny new Morgan in the palm of his hand.

Looking off up the road at nothing in particular, Sam slid the silver dollar into his shirt pocket and buttoned the flap, adding almost to himself, "Gettin' sloppy can get a man kilt mighty fast, especially if he's a gunslingin' outlaw on the run."

January 27, 1875

Chicago, Cook County, Illinois

Pinky Two Step

ALLAN J. PINKERTON SAT in his walnut-paneled office overlooking Lake Michigan, staring at two crumpled telegrams amidst the piles of papers burying his desk. Accepting a request by the Adams Express Company in 1874, his agency had taken on the task of rounding up the notorious James-Younger Gang. Since that time, one thing after another had gone wrong. The first news that had come in March, roughly a year ago, was good, they had taken down John Younger. It turned out to be a small victory, considering the operation had also taken the lives of two good men and allowed a bigger fish, Jim Younger, to get away clean.

The Boonville robbery where three Pinkerton agents had been wounded in a botched ambush, coming only days after the shootout with John and Jim Younger, had been a blow and a hard one to take. Now it seemed Allan Pinkerton had an even bigger political disaster on his hands.

The first telegram laying before him had informed him of how an assault on the James family farm in Clay County, Missouri, an operation the agency had been planning for months, had gone very badly. It seems Jesse and Frank James had not been home when local Pinkerton operatives, in a botched effort to flush out the desperadoes, used an exploding flare, mistakenly maiming the James brothers' mother, Zerelda, and killing an eight-year old half-brother, Archie Samuel. Should the media ever get hold of the truth behind the raid, they would have a heyday attacking Allan Pinkerton. The reputation of the Pinkerton National Detective Agency would be greatly damaged. There was even the chance a charge of murder could end up being filed.

Pinkerton's frown turned skyward into a broad smile when he considered how the information contained in the second telegram might provide the break his agency needed, a way to tidy things up once and for all. According to the telegram, a tip about the outlaw Billy Chadwell had been received several years ago by Jack Philips, a Pinkerton operative in Missouri. The Pinkerton Agency, with no specific contract to track down the James-Younger Gang at the time, had set the tip aside. Even so, what made the tip interesting after all these years was that it had come from a highly decorated former Union Army intelligence officer.

The original report indicated that the tip had come from Leroy Thompson, a southerner who was known to be a shady character and often involved in questionable business dealings. What a classified Union Army file said, which now sat on Pinkerton's desk, was that Leroy Thompson had been a spy for the Union Army during the war. Further digging in Army files had revealed that Leroy Thompson was none other than William Barton, a Union Army soldier who had served valiantly and who had been decorated for bravery under fire on several occasions during the war.

Why Barton had chosen to use the name Leroy Thompson when he provided his tip about Billy Chadwell to Jack Philips, and why Barton was still using his Leroy Thompson alias two years after the war would, as far as Allan Pinkerton was concerned, remain a mystery, despite evidence from additional investigations into the dealings of Leroy Thompson having turned up a cattle rustling swindle that had bilked a group of East Coast investors led by a Mr. Theodor Jeffers of Boston, Massachusetts out of $13,000 around the same time the tip was received. Further investigation revealed the cattle had ended up being returned to the rightful owner, while Mr. Jeffers had ended up returning to Boston empty-handed with neither cattle nor cash. Pinkerton and his agency had no bone to pick with William Barton and likely never would. As far as the Allan Pinkerton was concerned and as far as any official records that might survive would ever reveal, the tip had come from one Leroy Thompson, whereabouts unknown.

What interested Pinkerton was that the original tip from Leroy Thompson was a tip he now knew had come from a reliable informant. A man who had risked his life to serve his country as a spy during the war. A man whose word Pinkerton felt he could trust.

Thompson's tip involved a plan by the James-Younger Gang to take down a bank somewhere in the north and that this was to be their big score, the mother of all robberies, the one that would make them all rich. Before they pulled off this big job, Billy Chadwell told Leroy Thompson, the gang would contact him. The tip was simple: stake out Billy, take down the James-Younger Gang. Pinkerton liked the simplicity of the plan, especially considering all the trouble more complex planning had created in recent years.

The *coup de grace*, the thing that made the tip even more valuable, was the fact that the James-Younger Gang had yet to rob a bank outside of the South or north of any border state. Though there had been rumors that the James-Younger Gang had robbed the bank in Corydon, Iowa on June 3, 1871, the fact was, no one knew for sure who the desperadoes had been. Though Clell Miller, a known member of the James-Younger Gang, had been tried for the robbery, he had been acquitted, leaving only a cold trail on any further suspects. A field report from Louisville, Kentucky, coincidently posted on the same date as the Corydon robbery, seemed to confirm the robbery couldn't have been the work of the James-Younger Gang. According to the report, Dan Bogan, a notorious gunslinger, famous for his quickdraw, had been killed in a gunfight at the Bixby's Saloon in downtown Louisville that same day. The gunfight had been witnessed by Mr. Robert Mondale, the owner of the saloon, and no fewer than twenty other patrons, who swore to a man, it had been a fair fight and the winner had been none other than Cole Younger. The report further stated that as a result, the gunfight had made Cole Younger one of the fastest men alive.

As further confirmation, the Corydon robbery had netted the bandits only $40,000, a large sum but a sum far short of the bonanza the James-Younger Gang was hunting for in a bank somewhere up north. Though it was known that the gang had robbed a train in Adair, Iowa in 1873, the robbery had netted only $3,000, an embarrassment for the likes of the James-Younger Gang. Considering everything, Pinkerton was confident that the gang had yet to rob a bank up north. If they were still planning on taking one down, believing it would deliver them with their motherlode, Leroy Thompson's tip might still be the Pinkerton Agency's best lead to finally take down the James-Younger Gang, once and for all.

Pinkerton had already sent word to operatives in Jackson County, Missouri to stake out Billy Chadwell. In the meantime, he knew he would have to deal with the blowback and the negative public sentiment that had been whipped up in the aftermath of the raid on the James family farm and its resulting debacle. The agency had already scrubbed their records of any evidence of their planning for the raid and had moved to ensure anyone involved was taken care of one way or another. The last thing Pinkerton needed was to have his reputation tarnished by a bunch of marauding outlaws now that the U.S. Department of Justice had outsourced their Internal Investigating Unit to the Pinkerton National Detective Agency.

Indeed, it had been Pinkerton's newly acquired access to military and government archives that had uncovered the identity of Leroy Thompson. The power he had gained in becoming the keeper of all secrets was something he never wanted to lose. He knew the sooner he crushed the James-Younger Gang, the better. He also knew failure was no longer an option.

December 25, 1875

Lizard Creek, Webster County, Iowa

Joy to the World

"WATCH ME, PA, WATCH me," Johnny cried out as he came riding his pony, holding the reins in one hand and twirling a lariat over his head with the other. A little sheep was running ahead of the pony and Johnny was trying his hand at being a cowboy. Just as they came by the house, Johnny threw the lariat, catching the sheep around the neck. He quickly looped the end of the rope around his saddle horn and jumped off his pony, pulling on the rope and following it down to the struggling animal while his pony backed up, keeping the rope taut. He soon grabbed two of the sheep's legs on the same side and flipped the animal onto its side and then tipped it up on its back, all four legs pointing toward the sky. Johnny then pretended to twirl a piece of short rope around the gathered up outstretched legs and clapped his hands together when he finished like he had seen rodeo cowboys do.

"Great job, son. You are getting better all the time," Bill yelled, proud of his soon to be eight-year-old son. Alda had also grown and had already become quite the little lady herself, helping her ma in the kitchen and around the house. Kids seemed to grow up in the blink of an eye, he thought. He and Lucy had hoped to have more children by now, but things had not worked out that way. Bill wished with all his heart for a third child soon. His hope was that Johnny and Alda would have a baby brother before the next Christmas. He and Lucy were not as ambitious as the Waites, but had agreed when Johnny was born, it would be nice to have at least six or seven children. They had also agreed the nation was young and growing with endless possibilities. It needed strong frontier people who were ready, willing, and able to build its future. They wanted their children to play their part.

It seemed that months would go by without a thought of the James-Younger Gang until Bill would hear of yet another robbery or killing or both. Looking at Johnny reminded Bill that almost nine years had passed since Lucy and he had made their midnight flight north. Though he had come to feel relatively secure in Lizard Creek, he knew after his close shave in Louisville that Cole Younger would never give up his search for Leroy Thompson and his sweetheart, Lucy Breeden. Cole's burning desire for Lucy was not the only thing that drove him, his pride and his honor as a southern gentleman made it all but certain that he would never give up his quest for retribution.

To take his mind off his daily concerns, Bill had become an avid reader and tried to keep up with recent events. Beyond catching a story about James-Younger Gang exploits now and again, there were many other exciting developments Bill liked to follow. In just a few months, America would begin to celebrate the 100th anniversary of the signing of the Declaration of Independence. Wilber—always the science enthusiast—had shared with Bill everything he had read about the Centennial Exhibition to be held in Philadelphia, Pennsylvania from May 10 to November 10, 1876. Many new discoveries and contraptions were to be unveiled at the exhibition. Bill was excited about learning more. He was very much looking forward to celebrating the Fourth of July in Fort Dodge, as many special events were being planned. The coming American Centennial year was shaping up to be an exciting one.

He also had followed with interest the news reports coming out of the Dakota Territory over the past year and a half. The whole nation was still abuzz with the news that gold had been discovered in French Creek in the Black Hills of Dakota on July 27, 1874 during the Custer Expedition which surveyed the region's mineral deposits for the first time. Subsequent discoveries of larger gold deposits in Deadwood Gulch in the northern Black Hills had set off a full-fledged gold rush, as miners with gold fever soon flooded into the Black Hills. The rush was still ongoing, with more and more reports of gold in the Black Hills and more and more men ready to risk everything to strike it rich. Like the California gold rush in the 1840s, Bill suspected the gold rush into the Black Hills would eventually open new lands up for pioneer settlement in western Dakota and the Black Hills region. Bill was excited to hear the news, thinking if he had been a younger man seeking a fresh chance to make his fortune, he might have joined the Black Hills gold rush himself.

As he watched little Johnny play cowboy, he was certain by the time Johnny was old enough to head west, in not so many years, those new lands might well be open for settlement. The adventure of carving out a new life in such a land excited Bill. He hoped his children would find it as irresistibly appealing as he did. He believed at that moment that the Barton family in its march westwards would stake its claim in the Dakota Territory one day.

After putting Johnny's pony back in the stable and stowing his gear, Bill and Johnny returned to the house. As they walked through the front door, they were met by all the festive scents and spicy aromas of the Christmas holiday. In the corner of the main room was a huge spruce Christmas tree decorated with candles, gay-colored ribbons, candy canes, homemade ornaments, and strings of popcorn and cranberries. Tucked under and around the tree the night before, by the jolly ol' elf Saint Nick himself, were brightly colored presents of every size and shape all tied with colorful ribbons waiting until after Christmas Dinner for their owners to rip them open, as was the Barton custom. Fresh bows of holly were draped on the fireplace mantle with a large finely crafted pinecone wreath situated at the center of the decorative display. Lucy and Alda had worked on the wreath for over a month and were convinced it would become a family heirloom one day. A huge golden-brown turkey set steaming in the middle of the dining table, surrounded by bowls of cranberry sauce, sweet potatoes, sliced candied beets, bread crumb stuffing, brown gravy, mash potatoes, and green beans. A large heap of steaming fresh buns and a dish of fresh butter filled out the menu.

Taking in the festive scene and the fine spread laid out on the table, Bill was confident no one would be going hungry in the Barton household this Christmas. For many years, the Bartons and Waites had shared the Christmas dinner ritual together. This year, the Waites had traveled back to Illinois to spend Christmas with Nancy's parents, who had been wanting to meet their growing herd of grandchildren. Bill dreamed that one day his children would also come to know their only living grandparent. He hoped that this would be their last Christmas without Pappy.

"Pa, look at the pie I baked!" Alda said as she marched into the main room holding a piping hot cinnamon and nutmeg spiced pumpkin pie. A freshly baked pecan pie and bowl of sugar plums had already been set on the side table, where Alda placed the pumpkin pie before running to give her pa a big hug.

"Christmas is my most favorite time," she said, her eyes twinkling with delight.

"Mine too, princess," Bill admitted. He had always loved how special the day really was.

There was no other day during the year where all men set their differences aside and gathered in peace and love. He recalled that even during the war years, the fighting had stopped on Christmas Day. He was pleased the federal government had finally made Christmas a national holiday in 1870. It seemed strange the holiday had never been officially recognized, considering the country had been predominately settled by Christians since the pilgrims' first landing at Plymouth Rock. He held no malice toward any other religion and felt all major religions should have their holiest day officially recognized. And though he was not a deeply religious man himself, he believed each man had a soul and that religion could provide a man who had lost his way with a moral compass to help him find his way back to his fellow men.

"Let's eat! I'm starved," Johnny said in a stout little voice. He had been practicing roping dogies all morning and was one little cowpoke who had worked up a man-sized appetite.

"Me too," Bill chimed in with a broad grin on his face.

"Me three," Alda cried out, giggling at her little play on words, something she had heard her pa say on more than a few occasions.

"Me four," Lucy added as she entered the main room from the kitchen while taking off her apron and brushing flour powder off her dress. Enjoying the play on words and the fun of just being silly together, they all shared a hearty laugh as they took their seats at the table.

Bill once again took everything in and looked from one smiling face to the next and knew he was, without a doubt, the luckiest man on earth. He had put his outlaw days behind him and prayed they would stay behind him and never catch up. In the back of his mind a nagging thought remained silent, but not dormant. Bill couldn't help but wonder where Cole Younger was and whether he, like other men, rested on this day of peace and love. He also wondered when the Barton family would finally be rid of the threat Cole Younger posed.

"Before we slice the turkey, let's pray," Lucy said as she looked at Bill. Bill could tell that even on this happy occasion, Lucy too was still haunted by thoughts of Cole and the threat he posed. With that, Bill folded his hands in front of him on the edge of the table and Lucy and the children followed suit.

"Come Lord Jesus be thou our guest and let this food to us be blessed. Amen," Bill recited the mealtime prayer he had memorized from childhood. Besides the Lord's Prayer, it was the only prayer he had memorized word for word.

"Amen," Lucy, Johnny, and Alda all said in unison.

"Now let's eat!" Johnny said breaking the spell, not wanting to wait another second to start digging in.

"Now you're talkin'," Bill said as he took up the carving knife and started to slice up the turkey. Plates were soon flying around the table as Lucy helped dip up the gravy. The holiday feast had begun.

Christmas had always been the one holiday when the Youngers tried to spend a little time with family and friends. The year before, wanting to catch up with Jim and Belle Reed, Cole and his brothers had planned to spend the Christmas holiday at the Reed Ranch on Younger Bend near Stigler, Oklahoma, until they learned that in April 1874, Jim and Belle had failed in their attempted robbery of the Austin-San Antonio stagecoach, leading to a relentless manhunt which ended in Jim Reed being killed in Paris, Texas that August. Belle, now on the run and with a bounty on her head, was said to be holed up somewhere in Indian Territory. Rumors also had it that since Jim's death, Belle had taken up with the horse thief Sam Starr, a well-known Cherokee outlaw. Learning the news, the Youngers had decided to steer clear of Younger Bend and had spent the holiday in Missouri.

When Christmas rolled around again, Cole and his brothers thought they would try to look up Belle now that things had cooled off. Rather than hunting for her in Indian Territory, they decided to visit her father's place in Texas, hoping Belle might also be down that way for the holidays. Once again, they were forced to change their plans. This time it was the Youngers themselves who were sent on the run from a well-armed gang of bounty hunters who had staked out the Shirley place in hopes of ambushing members of the James-Younger Gang who all had hefty bounties on their heads, bounties that would be paid dead or alive. Before splitting up to elude their relentless pursuers, the brothers had agreed to meet up south of the border in Rio Bravo before heading back to Missouri.

Cole had been holed up in Rio Bravo just across the Rio Grande, in the state of Tamaulipas, for more than ten days with no sign of his brothers. In many ways, Cole was relieved he and Belle wouldn't be spending the holiday together. The truth was Cole had mixed feelings about being around Belle now that she was a widow. He knew he still loved Belle Shirley and that he always would. He also knew, with Jim Reed dead, he might have a chance to finally have Belle for himself, even if this meant gunning down Sam Starr or some other buckaroo who might try to stand in his way. Touching the diamond ring next to his heart reminded him that even if he could have Belle Shirley back, Lucy-belle Breeden was the only woman he now wanted to share his life with.

The little village of Rio Bravo was still licking its wounds from a recent skirmish with a large force of Texas Rangers, under the command of Capitan Leander McNelly, that had come across the border against U.S. War Department orders to recover cattle that had been rustled from several ranches in southern Texas. It had been widely known for many years that stolen Texas cattle had often found their way to the Las Cuevas Ranch run by the Mexican cattle baron Juan Flores Salinas. According to locals, when the dust settled, old man Salinas himself and over eighty of his vaqueros were dead and over a thousand head of cattle recovered and driven north back across the Rio Grande into Texas.

The November 1875 battle across the border had already come to be known as the Las Cuevas War. Cole had little interest in the incident other than the unsettling fact that heavily armed Texas Rangers had come across the border to enforce the law. Members of the James-Younger Gang often ran into Mexico to dodge the law and to let things cool off before returning north. Cole feared Mexico would no longer be the safe haven it had been.

It wasn't the first time Cole found himself in Mexico at Christmas time. He liked hiding out in Mexico but cared little for Mexican Christmas celebrations which seemed to go on forever. He knew the Mexicans celebrated the Christmas season from December 3 through February 2. He had ridden into Rio Bravo on December 12, the feast day of the Virgin, the end of the nine-day novena to the Virgin of Guadalupe, the patron saint of Mexico. The only thing Cole knew of these celebrations was that the Virgin of Guadalupe had appeared to Juan Diego, a devout Indian man, four times over this nine-day period in 1531.

In the following days, Cole had also witnessed the Las Posadas that included reenactments of the Christmas story where Joseph and Mary sought shelter prior to the birth of Jesus. He watched as the peregrinos, the pilgrims, were finally admitted into someone's home followed by a party with food and drink and games, including blindfolded children swinging sticks until they busted open large seven-pointed and animal-shaped pinatas. A stranger to these customs, Cole often found himself watching the children play as he touched the diamond ring hanging around his neck. At moments like these, Cole truly believed that when he finally got his Lucy-belle back, they and their children would also share many carefree Christmas holidays together one day.

Cole had noticed the number of poinsettias decorating the town had increased since the morning. He knew that the poinsettia was indigenous to Mexico and had come to be known as Flor de Noche Buena, the Christmas Eve Flower. He had also learned that the star-shaped leaf pattern symbolized the Star of Bethlehem and the red color the blood of Jesus. As he walked into the cantina, it finally dawned on him that tonight was Noche Buena, the good night, Christmas Eve. The place was nearly empty as Mexican families prepared to attend midnight mass before returning home to a late-night feast. A large bowl of hot Ponche Navideno, Mexican Christmas fruit punch, sat on the bar with cups nearby. Helping himself, Cole ladled up a full cup of punch. The drink was sweetened with dark-brown cane sugar and cinnamon sticks. The combined tastes of sliced apples, oranges, guavas, and tejocotes, the sweet and sour tasting fruit of the hawthorn tree, gave the drink a fruity, citrusy, sweet and sour tang. Cole stood at the bar while he drank down the cup of punch and had to grudgingly admit he liked the holiday treat. Dipping up a second cup of punch, Cole ordered a bottle of tequila.

A mariachi trio played in the corner of the cantina as Cole took a seat at a rickety wooden table. Sipping his cup of tequila-spiked Ponche Navideno, he took note that other than the mariachi trio and the bartender, the only other people in the cantina were a pair of well-worn senoritas dancing with a couple of drunken cowpunchers from north of the border. Watching the couples sway across a filthy sawdust-covered floor, Cole thought about Belle Shirley and Lucy-belle Breeden and how he hadn't been with a woman in far too long.

Without a word, Cole stood up and grabbed an arm of the younger and more shapely of the two senoritas as she swung by close to his table. With a quick jerk, he pulled her away from the embrace of her drunken cowpuncher.

"Hey, hombre. Get your own senorita," the cowpuncher barked as he grabbed the senorita's other arm, making her the prize in what had now become a human tug-of-war. The cowpuncher's boldness and his sudden move took Cole by surprise, igniting the fuse on Cole's explosive temper.

"Let go of the little senorita, or make your play, amigo," Cole said through clenched teeth. The cowpuncher was now the one caught by surprise as his liquor-soaked brain struggled to comprehend the swiftly shifting ground under his feet. Oblivious to the gravity of his situation, the cowpuncher's temper flared, blinding him to his better senses.

"Now listen mister, I had her first. The little senorita is mine," he said, boldly pulling on her arm hard with both hands, breaking Cole's grip.

"You called it, cowpuncher, if you want to keep her, make your play," Cole said, his eyes narrowed, his hand free and ready to draw.

The cowpuncher, feeling victorious in having won his woman back, spun her around like a top until she lit hard on her substantial bottom into a nearby chair. With confidence in the form of 150-proof tequila coursing through his veins, he made his play.

Cole's Colt flew out of his holster in a blur and barked three times before the man's pistol cleared leather. Dead before he hit the floor, the cowpuncher's eyes now stared into the abyss, never to see another Christmas. Silence reined over the cantina after the loud gunshots ceased to echo off its walls. Breaking the silence was the cowpuncher's friend who, suddenly having been snapped out of his tequila stupor, grabbed his rotund senorita around the waist and, using her considerable bulk as a kind of portly shield, pulled her backward out through the cantina's swinging doors and into the night without bothering to look back. As gun smoke drifted in the stale air, Cole quickly reloaded and holstered his pistol.

Though traditions might be different south of the border, a man still needed a warm body next to him on Christmas Eve, Cole thought. Looking down at the dead cowpuncher, his eyes wide with belated realization and his mouth twisted in a final grimace of pain, Cole filled his cup with tequila and poured it into the man's gaping mouth. "Merry Christmas my amigo, *Feliz Navidad*," he said as he laughed with abandon, his laughter echoing off the walls of the empty cantina, bringing joy to no one but himself. Flipping a twenty-dollar gold piece to the bartender, he motioned for him to dispose of the cowpuncher's body. He figured the bartender would be happy to do so after stripping it of any valuables. Considering recent events, no one in Rio Bravo would give a damn about what might have happened to an unknown gringo cowpuncher from somewhere north of the border.

Pulling his prize up out of her chair, he spun the shapely senorita around, taking in her many curves. *"Toca algunos villancicos,* Christmas carols, damn it! Something to dance to, *algo para bailar, comprendes?"* he yelled to the mariachi trio that had stood stock-still in the corner of the cantina like a row of wax museum statues since the first gunshot.

Digging three more twenty-dollar gold pieces out of his pocket, he tossed them into an open guitar case sitting in front of the trio. Cole clapped his hands and motioned for the trio to begin. Upon seeing the three twenty-dollar gold pieces now shining brightly in the bottom of the battered guitar case, every man in the trio knew this would be a very, very, very merry Christmas, if he could only live through the night to enjoy it. Having witnessed the deadly consequences for not following the orders of the crazy pistolero, the mariachi trio soon filled the cantina with the musical sounds of Christmas carols suitable for dancing.

Pressing the senorita's substantial and shapely body hard against his own, Cole began to sway around the empty cantina floor. *"Viva la Mexico! Viva la Senorita! Viva* my Christmas-belle!" Cole roared into the empty room with a forced laugh and a wild look on his face. The senorita with no chance nor place to run, stared at Cole with the look of utter dread and terror in her eyes. She knew her Christmas would be anything but a merry one.

August 30, 1876

Chicago, Cook County, Illinois

Hawks and Sparrows

THE MESSENGER HAD BEEN told the telegram he held in his hand was only for the eyes of Mr. Allan J. Pinkerton himself. The messenger was to let no one else even touch the envelope before it was delivered. As the messenger ran into the Pinkerton National Detective Agency headquarters, he wondered what could possibly be so secret and so important that he had even been instructed to take the back stairs rather than the newly installed rope-geared hydraulic elevator, which he loved to ride when he got a chance. Sweating by the time he reached the twentieth floor, he hurried down the long hallway to the corner office, the office of none other than Mr. Allan J. Pinkerton, the president and founder of the Pinkerton National Detective Agency. The boy dreamed that one day he too would be a Pinky. The fact that Pinkerton agents often worked undercover was exciting to a small boy, as a world of cloak and dagger exploits promised a life of mystery and intrigue.

He knocked before entering the president's office. The president's secretary, Miss Anne Johnson, a plump middle-aged woman in a dark corduroy dress with a starched white laced collar buttoned at the top, motioned for the boy to step forward. The boy looked at her round pinched face and was about to speak when she demanded, "Boy, don't just stand there, give me the envelope."

The boy stepping back a pace held the message tightly to his chest and said in his most serious and deepest voice, "I am sorry ma'am, but this message is for Mr. Allan J. Pinkerton his self. I was told to let no one else even touch it."

"Well, I am sure you can give it to me. I handle all of Mr. Pinkerton's messages," Anne retorted, holding out her plump little hand palm up.

"No ma'am, I can't let anyone have this message. I promised to hand it directly to Mr. Allan J. Pinkerton his self, no one else," the boy said, not giving in an inch.

After a long silent standoff with both parties frozen like insects in amber, Miss Johnson finally relented. "Very well then, follow me," she said as she tipped herself off her seat, her legs being too short to touch the floor when fully seated, and waddled to the door leading to Mr. Allan J. Pinkerton's inner office.

She tapped on the door twice and then entered with the boy in tow. "Mr. Pinkerton, excuse us, but the boy here has a message he insists he must deliver directly to your hands only," she said, more than a little peeved and perplexed.

Pinkerton, looking up from a pile of papers on his desk, immediately stopped what he was doing and asked the young boy to step forward. The boy, awestruck, stepped forward and handed the message with a shaky hand directly to the hand of Mr. Allan J. Pinkerton.

Pinkerton asked his secretary to leave. Once she was gone, he quickly opened the envelope and began reading its contents. As he read, a huge smile lit up his face. When he finished, he tucked the message into his suit jacket's inner lapel pocket. He then turned the full measure of his attention to the boy.

"Well, son, you just won yourself a well-earned bounty," Pinkerton said as he reached into one of his desk drawers and rifled through its contents. Finally coming up with what he was looking for, he flipped the boy a shiny Morgan silver dollar, dated 1874. The boy snatching the coin out of the air, put it into his shirt pocket, and buttoned the flap in a single move.

Little did the boy know that the dollar he now held secured in his shirt pocket had come from the latest James-Younger Gang bank robbery down in Boone County, Missouri. According to the field report, the dollar had been mistakenly left behind by the gang. It was the first time the gang had been sloppy enough to leave a clue about where they had met up after a robbery, which helped in the recovery of important bank bonds and records that had been buried by the gang nearby. The silver dollar had been wrapped in a short note that read:

As a token of luck, use this shiny silver dollar as bounty for the messenger who first brings you word that the James-Younger Gang has finally made a fatal mistake. Good hunting.

Best wishes for success, Sheriff Sam Jefferson

The boy couldn't believe his luck, as the tip was the biggest he had ever received. Thinking only of the shiny silver dollar buttoned safely in his shirt pocket, the boy didn't notice the confused and somewhat concerned look on the secretary's face as he passed Miss Johnson's desk. This was the first time she had been asked to leave Mr. Pinkerton's office before the messenger had gone.

The message in Pinkerton's jacket pocket confirmed that the James-Younger Gang had made "a fatal mistake," the outlaw Billy Chadwell was on the move. Charlie Pitts had come to Billy's place south of Westport and the two had ridden to Independence, Missouri together. They were now headed north into Iowa. Agents in Jackson County and in Clay County had reported sightings of both Cole Younger and Jesse James heading out of their places over a week ago, destinations unknown. Subsequent reports from the area indicated that Frank James and Jim and Bob Younger had also set out together on horseback the same day ol' Billy had taken to the road.

With so many gang members on the move and ol' Billy headed north, Pinkerton knew with certainty that Leroy Thompson's tip had finally borne fruit. Pinkerton alerted field agents stationed in the larger towns in Iowa, southern Illinois, and southern Minnesota to stake out the local banks and be on the lookout. The James-Younger Gang would strike a bank with sizable deposits somewhere in that three-state region within a week. He also instructed all Pinkerton agents to remain undercover and to shoot to kill. They were on no account to identify themselves as agents of the Pinkerton Agency. When the smoke clears on the operation, the public will need to believe that any shooting or killing by Pinkerton men was in fact the actions of ordinary civilians doing their civic duty to protect their town.

The Pinkerton Agency would admit no foreknowledge of any planned robbery and would take no credit for taking down the James-Younger Gang. Pinkerton wanted the agency to take no credit for any killing. His only goal was to take the gang down once and for all. He was sure the gang would hit somewhere in the targeted three-state region and that they would not risk riding too far from home. He felt certain the James-Younger Gang would soon meet their Waterloo.

September 3, 1876

Rockwell City, Calhoun County, Iowa

Too Close for Comfort

BILL HAD HEARD THAT John Rockwell and his wife Charlotte had just plat-ted a new town in the next county only a few miles west of Lizard Creek. He had dealt with John Rockwell on cattle business in the past and thought he would ride over to see how many folks had already settled in John's new town. Lucy asked him to see if they had any new merchants setting up shop. She was ever on the lookout for well-stocked sewing emporiums. With their third child on the way, Bill knew Lucy would need more swaddling cloth soon. Little Johnny had begged to ride along, but Lucy had vetoed the idea, saying that the long ride over and back would be too far for a boy of only eight years old. Bill had assured the boy he would be ready to ride on day trips with his pa when he was ten. Little Alda had also piped in saying she wanted to go too, until he promised her that he would bring back some of Mrs. Rockwell's famous homemade cookies. With thoughts of delicious cookies dancing in her head, she just smiled and waved goodbye, yelling as he parted, "Don't forget the cookies!"

Without a care in the world, Bill took in the sights as he rode into Calhoun County. After arriving at the new settlement of Rockwell City and talking with the Rockwells, it became clear the new town wouldn't be much to crow about for some time. The current population was less than fifty souls without many prospects for that number to grow rapidly. There were a few shops going up to cater to local farm folk. Unfortunately, there wasn't a sewing emporium among them.

Charlotte, always the consummate hostess, had served an early dinner for Bill's sake, knowing he would need to ride back to Lizard Creek before it got too late. During dinner, the conversation covered many topics of the day. John, like Bill, had been following stories about the Black Hills gold rush. They had both been surprised and saddened by news reports just a few months earlier in June 1876 of the death of General George Armstrong Custer, a well-known Civil War hero and Indian fighter, along with 210 7th Cavalry soldiers at the Battle of the Little Big Horn northwest of the Black Hills. Following Custer's death, Bill had read up on the 1868 Treaty of Fort Laramie that had given the Lakota Sioux Indians all the land in the Dakota Territory west of the Missouri River including the Black Hills. The Sioux under Sitting Bull and Crazy Horse were resisting the rush of white men into the Black Hills, land they saw as their people's sacred home territory. Bill and John both agreed the gold rush had ripped open these lands and that in a very short time the number of emigrants flowing west would inevitably crisscross the Dakota Territory with railroads and where only buffalo now roamed, new towns would sprout out of the prairie. They both knew the Indians would resist, possibly for years, as would any people whose lands had been invaded. Both men knew, however, that there would be no way to hold back the mounting tide of history or the belief in the nation's manifest destiny.

Whether it was right or just was difficult to judge on every count. All they knew was that more people every year were moving west, and more were following right behind them. There would be no way to stem the nation's relentless push ever westward. Bill told John and Charlotte that he wanted his children to be part of that westward march. He wanted the Barton family to lay claim to their destiny, which since the first Barton to set foot in the new world had been to push ever westward. The Rockwells felt very much the same. Their desire to stake their claim had been the reason they had planned a new town and why they hoped their children would push further west as the nation grew to fill up the land.

Though Bill had hoped for an early start back, the two men's conversation had turned to politics, a topic both men loved to talk about, and one Bill couldn't resist. John supported the Republican candidate, Governor Rutherford B. Hayes of Ohio, who he thought would be the best man to carry on President Grant's policies. Bill also supported Hayes and couldn't help railing against the Democrat candidate, Governor Samuel J. Tilden of New York, who he believed would withdraw federal troops from the South and end Reconstruction too soon, moves John also believed would be a disaster not only for the unity of the nation but for millions of newly freed slaves. Though John and Bill often agreed with one another, they had both thoroughly enjoyed their rousing political discussion. By the time the dust settled, Bill's departure had grown later than he had planned.

What neither man could have guessed at the time was that the upcoming presidential election results would be contested, with Tilden winning the popular vote and Hayes, after much wrangling, winning the electoral college by one vote. In a smoke-filled backroom deal, Tilden would agree Hayes could become president on one very important condition: federal troops would be withdrawn from the South and Reconstruction ended. As it would turn out, regardless of the winner, be it Democrat or Republican, the outcome of the 1876 election would make little difference to millions of freed slaves, as their newly-won civil rights were destined to be lost for nearly a hundred years, either way.

Finally saying his farewells and gathering up a fat packet of fresh baked cookies that Charlotte had made up special for the kids, Bill pulled himself away and rode out of Rockwell City as the sun slid toward the horizon in the west. Riding east, he couldn't help looking back from time to time to enjoy the sunset which painted the clouds in the western sky with brush strokes of crimson and gold. With the last fading rays of the sun, darkness spread across the land. Bill was happy he didn't have too far to go. Bill nudged his horse into a slow and easy trot, the moonless night making it difficult to see very far. Just as he came up a small wash near the west bank of Lizard Creek, he heard the pounding sound of hoofbeats coming up hard behind him. Startled, Bill's horse whinnied, throwing up its head, its ears rotating back and forth.

Several horses replied, the sound of their hoofbeats getting closer. Bill wasn't quite sure what to think since hearing the hoofbeats of many hard charging riders in the middle of a moonless night was unusual. He knew it couldn't be the calvary from Fort Dodge, since it was widely known they were on maneuvers in the Dakota Territory.

The riders were almost upon him before he could make out any of their faces in the dark. To his horror, the first pair of eyes he found himself staring straight into were the piggy blood-shot eyes of Charlie Pitts. From the look on Charlie's face, Bill could see the man had recognized him instantly.

"Whoa!" Charlie howled, reining up his horse. "Hey Cole, I just ran into the ol' horse thief Leroy Thompson his self. Isn't he the low-down polecat who stole your woman?" Charlie yelled, signaling for the other riders, coming up behind him, to take a gander at his unexpected catch.

Out of the darkness the face of Cole Younger emerged, his eyes burning with hate. Not wishing to get further acquainted, Bill spurred his horse and lit out to the south as fast as his horse could gallop. He was sure Cole had gotten a good look at him and that the other Younger brothers were in the group. Behind him he could hear the confused commotion of men yelling to one another and horses crying out. The crack of a rifle echoed through the night followed by a sharp rebuke, "Hold your fire, boys, we need to take him alive!" Bill was in no doubt the order to hold fire had come from Cole Younger himself.

The single round, however, had found its mark; Bill had been stuck in the shoulder with such force it had nearly thrown him off his horse. Bleeding and confused, all he could think of was getting as far away from Lizard Creek as his horse could carry him. He plunged south into the night, praying that though they may catch him, Cole Younger would never lay a hand on his precious Lucy or their children.

The James-Younger Gang had decided to come up through Fort Dodge, Iowa on their way to Mankato, Minnesota, the location of their long-dreamed-of El Dorado. Jesse had thought the route would be a straight shot north and would keep the gang off the main roads. Normally the gang would steer clear of Fort Dodge. Jesse however had learned that the Calvary garrisoned at Fort Dodge was out on maneuvers in the Dakota Territory, making it unlikely the gang would have any trouble passing through the area.

After their unexcepted run-in with Leroy Thompson, the gang broke into two groups. The Youngers, led by Cole, lit out after Leroy Thompson. The rest of the gang with Jesse at the head continued the journey north. After crossing the Des Moines River near Fort Dodge, the plan was for everyone to meet up just south of Blue Earth, Minnesota by first light come morning.

Jesse knew all about the long-running grudge Cole had with Leroy Thompson but didn't want Cole's love life to interfere with the gang's plans. Cole and Jesse had talked about Lucy Breeden and Leroy Thompson on more than one occasion over the years. Everyone in the gang knew Cole would never rest until he had killed Leroy Thompson and got his woman back. Jesse could never understand why any man would lose his mind over any one woman. He always figured there were plenty of good women to choose from. Jesse himself had married his cousin less than two years ago with the hope she would give him the sons he had always wanted. Little Jesse junior was now just a year old and Jesse had high hopes for the boy. Turning his mind from Cole's troubles, Jesse concentrated on the job ahead as he continued to lead his now-diminished ranks on their long ride north.

A horse's nicker pierced the moonless inky-black silence like the point of a razor-sharp lance. The unmistakable sound bristled the hairs on Bill's sweat-drenched neck, sending his heart pounding in his chest like a caged beast. Bill laid on his horse, cupping its head with both hands, firmly clamping off any unguarded reply. He judged the nicker had come from the thicket off to his left no more than a hundred yards behind him. He had no way to know if his relentless pursuer knew Bill was close or was simply trying to see what he might be able to flush out of the shadows.

The rider and his nickering horse continued to pick their way through the brush first one way, then the other, coming ever closer with every step. The rider made no attempt to silence his winded pony. Bill had ridden hard for hours to stay ahead of his pursuers until his horse could go no further. Laying him down in the brush, Bill had hoped to rest and, God willing, to let his pursuers ride on by. That plan seemed like a good one at the time, but now he wondered how his pursuers seemed to always know his every move in advance. When he had doubled back, his pursuers were ready. When he had rode up a small stream to cover his tracks, his pursuers had followed without missing a beat. He even tried using livestock to shield his movements; once again, his pursuers hadn't been fooled. Hiding in the shadows, he feared all his running would soon come to a violent end.

Bill knew if he let his horse up and tried to face down his pursuers or if he now tried to make a run for it in the open, he would be cut down without mercy. It was well-known the Youngers all carried Winchesters that they could rapid-fire with deadly accuracy at a full gallop. The wound in his shoulder reminded him that the stories of their shooting abilities were no exaggeration. His only hope was for the rider to pass by close enough that he might take him down from behind with the wicked razor-sharp blade of the knife he had acquired back in Louisville, Kentucky from the late Jacob O'Leary. Killing a Younger was his worst possible option. If he did, the Youngers would redouble their efforts to pursue him to the gates of hell and beyond to even the score. If pushed, however, he would do it without hesitation. As with so many condemned men, Bill found religion and prayed to all that was holy for his pursuer to pass by quietly, so he could ride out when the coast was clear. The course history would now take depended solely on the whims of a nickering pony and its relentless rider.

A barking growl seemed to come out of nowhere, "Cole, Cole, over here! Bobby thinks he found his trail and traces of fresh blood." The rider reined up less than twenty feet from where Bill and his jet-black steed lay motionless in the brush. One downward glance and the rider would find his prey. Bill froze as time slowed to a standstill.

"On my way!" yelled the rider as he swung his horse around, spurring its flanks to quicken its pace. Bill instantly recognized the voice of the rider as belonging to the natural-born killer, Cole Younger himself. The jingle of tack and thumping of hoofbeats faded into the distance.

Voices drifted on the wind as Bill heard Cole Younger and other men discussing their next moves. One of the men had a high-pitched voice that carried well in the cool night air. Bill could clearly hear him outline the gang's future plans.

"Alright, if Mankato is a bust, we'll go on to Northfield. Either way, we still all get rich, right?" said the high-pitched rider, his remark followed by muffled sounds of laughter.

After that the riders seemed to move further off, their voices becoming fainter until he heard only silence. Bill was in no doubt he had heard the names of the towns the gang intended to strike the next day. He knew he needed to alert Mankato and Northfield as soon as possible. He had no time to waste if he hoped to get ahead of the gang's plans.

Not hearing any sounds from any riders for a long time, Bill lifted his hands from his horse's head, allowing the steed to blow heavily through its nose. For a long moment they lay quietly as both man and beast breathed deeply, allowing the tension to pour out of them. They lay there together as though they were fellow travelers who had finally found shelter from a raging storm. Bill slowly lifted his head above the brush line. A cool breeze flowed over the tops of the grass as Bill strained to hear any signs of his pursuers. The silence around him bloomed back to life in a cacophony of buzzing and chirping sounds which rang out from every direction. Bill realized he hadn't been the only living thing that had feared discovery and possible death.

Bill slowly got to his feet, bringing his horse up with him. His horse nickered and blew through its nostrils as it shook its head from side to side. The wound in his shoulder throbbed and waves of pain radiated down his back. To slow the bleeding, he packed the wound with dry grass and wrapped it the best he could with his trusty bandana. He knew the bullet would need to be taken out soon. Quickly cinching up his saddle, Bill swung up on his horse and headed north.

Having finally caught scent of their prey, the Youngers would never give up searching for Leroy Thompson and the whereabouts of Lucy Breeden. It was a matter of honor for Cole Younger, the honor of an aggrieved southern gentleman. The kind of honorable chivalry that had driven more than one man to kill another. Bill knew he would need more than a little luck to stop Cole or one of his brothers from upholding the family honor. He would have to use all the wits and skills he had honed as a spy during the war to evade the vengeances of the Youngers. Bill had wanted to believe he had buried Leroy Thompson back in Missouri; he had long since come to appreciate that burying the past wasn't so easy. Like his encounter with Jacob O'Leary in Louisville, his encounter tonight with Charlie Pitts and the James-Younger Gang had reminded him that the past had a way of not staying buried.

As Bill rode through the night, he could only think of Lucy. She had changed the course of his life since that day on the banks of the Little Platte River. If love at first sight was ever possible, Bill knew it had happened that day when their eyes first met. Motionless, they had stared at each other for what seemed like an eternity, though he knew it had been only an instant. Her eyes had burnt through to his soul and he knew in that fleeting moment she too had felt the same about his eyes and her soul.

Had he known when he first stumbled upon Lucy that she was Cole Younger's sweetheart, his better senses might have told him to hightail it out of there as quickly as his horse could gallop. Dazed by her beauty, Bill's only desire had been to know more about the precious creature who stood before him. His God-given senses to steer clear of danger had simply abandoned him.

It was only after he had talked with her and fallen head over heels for her and arranged to meet her the next day that he had learned her name and the potentially violent implications that came with it. Though Louisville had been a close call, until this night he had never appreciated fully the ramifications of what he had done and where it might lead.

Now that Cole Younger knew what he looked like and where to look for him, he knew his only chance was to grab his family and run. With Johnny and Alda still so young and Lucy expecting so soon, he also knew running was no longer an option. If he couldn't run, he would need to stand and fight. He knew if it came to that, his odds of surviving were next to none.

Learning where the gang was headed had, however, tilted the advantage back in his favor. He was excited about his prospects for taking down the gang, and in doing so, ridding Lucy and himself of Cole Younger and his brothers once and for all. If he had to stand and fight, he was determined to launch his own attack on Cole before Cole had the chance to hunt him down. Striking Cole first was the only way. What made this plan even better was that it would be the last thing Cole Younger would ever expect, the prey turning the tables on the hunter.

As he rode north, he surveyed the skies for a sign. The night air was crystal clear, and the North Star shone brighter than at any time he could remember. Looking behind him, he was mesmerized by the multitude of fireflies that lit up and swirled off into the darkness in the wake of his galloping horse. These signs made him confident he had chosen the right course and that though there was much uncertainty, he would need to stay the course to its fiery end.

The Youngers continued to comb the area for over an hour, coming up with nothing. Frustrated, Cole and his brothers finally headed north to join the rest of the gang. Tomorrow would be their big day. Cole knew Leroy Thompson might flee the area during their robbery up north. He also finally knew what Leroy Thompson looked like and generally where he had been hiding out all these years. Cole was convinced he would be able to track the bastard down. Clutching the diamond wedding ring he hung around his neck close to his heart for so many years, he was more certain than ever that Lucy-belle would be his again, and very soon.

September 4, 1876

Mankato, Blue Earth County, Minnesota

Best-Laid Plans

IN ADVANCE OF THE gang's arrival, Jesse and Cole had scouted several possible bank targets as far north as St. Paul the week before. Despite the banks in Red Wing, St. Peter, and Northfield all looking like tempting secondary targets, they had returned to their original plan of knocking over the First National Bank in Mankato, believing it was where the carpetbaggers hid their cash, the place where they would strike the motherlode. They would hit the Frist National Bank in Northfield as a fallback, if Mankato turned out to be a bust. Like Mankato, they suspected the bank in Northfield also held piles of ill-gotten Reconstruction money, more than any of the other options. The men agreed that either bank, Mankato or Northfield, would net the gang the bonanza they sought.

After confirming the gang's targets, the two men had ridden back south into Iowa to meet up with the rest of the gang in the town of Carroll in Carroll County, Iowa, near the switching station of the Chicago and Northwestern Railroad. On the morning of September 3 after everyone had arrived, the gang soon got down to business, confirming the final plan and duties for each gang member for their assault on the Mankato bank. They also discussed a plan for the Northfield bank, though Jesse seemed less enthusiastic about going over all the details for Northfield, clearly hoping there would be no need to worry about any fallback plan.

Wanting to pass by Fort Dodge under cover of darkness, the James-Younger Gang, finally riding together as one had waited until afternoon to ride north out of Carroll County, Iowa for Blue Earth County, Minnesota. They had decided to cross the Des Moines River at Fort Dodge and ride from there in a straight shot north to Mankato, Minnesota. The unexpected appearance of Leroy Thompson had blown up their original plan, forcing Jesse to ride north with only half the gang in tow, the Younger brothers having followed Cole when he lit out after the fleeing Leroy Thompson.

Jesse watched the eastern sky grow brighter as dawn slowly stole the sky from the night. Jesse and his half of the gang had arrived at the planned rendezvous in Blue Earth County, Minnesota early enough to allow everyone to catch a little badly-needed shuteye. In the dim rose-colored light of the early dawn, the men were now up and checking their weapons and stowing their gear. They would soon be ready to make the final ride to Mankato. Jesse wondered when and even if the Youngers would join them. He knew when the Youngers did finally arrive, they wouldn't be in the best of condition nor would their horses, considering none of them would have had any rest for nearly twenty-four hours. Though the Mankato bank seemed like an easy enough target, Jesse knew things had a way of going haywire when you least expected it.

"Riders comin," Frank James called out as he walked over to where Jesse sat on a rocky outcropping along the banks of the Blue Earth River, two miles south of Mankato.

"Well, at least they got here before daybreak," Jesse said in a sour tone. His words had no more than cleared his lips when the leading arc of the sun's disk popped up over the edge of the eastern horizon. Jesse could only shake his head and wonder how the Leroy Thompson incident might have put more than a little kink in their best-laid plans.

Bill had doubled back and headed north while the Youngers continued to comb the brush for any sign of Leroy Thompson. There was a risk in riding north in the same direction the Youngers would come; however, Bill had figured he would be able to stay ahead of the Youngers. One advantage he had was that he knew the local terrain better than them. He also figured he would have a good hour's head start, knowing Cole would be unable to give up his search for Leroy Thompson easily now that he had the scent of his prey and was so close to a kill.

Outrunning the Youngers and avoiding a run-in with Jesse and the rest of the gang, Bill arrived in Mankato less than an hour before daybreak.

He was lightheaded and exhausted from loss of blood when he stumbled into the sheriff's office. He recounted the story he had concocted on his way to Mankato. Bill didn't want anyone to suspect that he knew any of the outlaws who had waylaid him or any of the James-Younger Gang, nor did he want them to suspect he had been the infamous cattle rustler Leroy Thompson known widely in Missouri and in the South after the war.

Careful to warn the town without providing too many details about how he obtained the information, Bill shared his story with Sheriff Bob Butts and several of his deputies. The version of events according to Bill's story was that he had been bushwhacked by desperadoes near Fort Dodge. Wounded by one of the bandits during his escape, he had been chased all over northern Iowa. During the chase he had overheard one of the gang members say they needed to forget about chasing some dirt-poor farmer, because they had a rich bank to rob in Mankato or Northfield. Bill guessed that the gang would hit the Mankato bank soon, maybe even today. When asked, Bill had said he was not sure how many gang members there might be but thought he had seen seven or eight riders.

Upon hearing Bill's story, Sheriff Butts ordered his deputies to double the guard on the bank and to keep a sharp lookout. He also ordered them to double-check the positioning of added security around town. The sheriff shared that he had received a confidential official alert about a possible bank robbery in one of the towns in this area only a few days ago. In anticipation, the sheriff had hired extra deputies in recent days. He was determined not to let any low-down outlaws rob his bank. He said Northfield and the other towns in the area had also doubled security in recent days, having all received the same alert. It seemed from Bill's story that the bandits would hit either Mankato or Northfield. Sheriff Butts assured Bill he would send an additional warning to the sheriff in Northfield just in case.

During the recounting of his story, the town doctor, Dr. Carl Masters, had been called to look at Bill's shoulder wound. Bill was quickly escorted to the doctor's office soon after telling his story.

"We'll have to get that bullet out and stop the bleeding as soon as possible. It doesn't look like the bullet is lodged in any bone, so things should go well enough. It's going to hurt like hell, though," Doc Masters said as he probed the wound.

Bill winced as he laid face-down on the operating table. He was told by a female assistant they would administer chloroform. Before he could protest, the assistant had already placed a cup-like device over his nose and mouth.

"Alright, Mr. Barton, just breath in and out slowly and count to one hundred," the assistant cooed into his ear.

The Youngers had no more than rode in and rejoined the gang when Jesse told them not to get too comfortable and to be ready to mount up again as soon as they had a short rest and a quick cup of coffee. The Youngers, visibly trail-weary, agreed with Jesse without protest, saying only that Leroy had given them the slip. Angrily, Cole said he would take care of Leroy after the robbery and added that no one else needed to get involved. Cole's attempt to reassure Jesse and the rest of the gang that they needn't worry about Leroy Thompson was received without comment. It was clear no one in the gang was in the mood to hear any more about Cole Younger's long-lost sweetheart or the bastard who stole her.

Jesse had the gang split up into two groups so they could enter the town from both ends. One group would ride to the livery stable. From there they would monitor the Main Street from the hayloft which overlooked the main square. Jesse would wave a red flag if the other group was to enter the town and a white flag if something was amiss, in which case everyone was to withdraw to the second rendezvous spot south of Northfield. Should this happen, they would cross Mankato off their list.

Getting to Mankato, Jesse, Charlie Pitts, and Bob and Jim Younger entered the livery stable from the rear. Jesse was immediately suspicious when he spied several men up in the hayloft playing cards. Though having men around the livery stable this time of day seemed a little odd, it wasn't out of the ordinary. Cowpunchers often found a quiet place to play a game of poker. Jesse decided to go ahead and send Charlie unarmed down the boardwalk for a look-see. Charlie returned after twenty minutes and reported that there were armed men inside the doorways of nearly every establishment on Main Street.

Jesse, not wanting to give up, asked Bobby, the youngest of the Younger brothers, to also take off his holster and to go on down to the bank and to look inside. The advantage of sending Bobby was that he had the most angelic face and highest-pitched voice of any of the gang members by a mile. Sending him unarmed made him look even more innocent.

"Bobby, when you get up to the counter, hand this ten-dollar bill to the teller and say your pa needs to have some Morgans around to pay part-time farm hands," Jesse instructed Bobby, handing him a folded ten-dollar bill. "Beyond saying please and thank you, don't say anything else to anyone," Jesse continued, worried the kid might say something to set off an alarm.

Bobby returned in short order with ten Morgan silver dollars coins bulging in his left front pants pocket and a worried look on his face.

"The bank has three armed guards. I've never see'd men packin' so much hardware. Everyone seemed kind'a tense," Bobby reported as one of the heavy coins unceremoniously slid down his leg and out of his left pant cuff and rolled on its edge until it bumped into a fresh steaming pile of roadside apples and then fell over on its side, tails up.

"Well boys, I think that sums it up," Jesse said motioning with his chin at the shiny silver dollar coin lying face down next to a pile of horse shit. "Looks like you got a hole in your pocket Bobby, best get them silver dollars tucked away in your saddlebags. We're gettin' the hell out of here," Jesse added matter-of-factly as he turned on the heel of his boot and headed for his horse.

Cole, Frank, Billy Chadwell, and Clell Miller waited for a signal, but none came. They decided to retreat to a well-sheltered ravine with good brush cover just off the main road leading to town until they received word from Jesse. It was obvious something was amiss in Mankato.

After nearly an hour Jesse rode in. He filled them in on the situation in Mankato and told them that Jim, Charlie, and Bobby were already headed for the rendezvous spot south of Northfield. To avoid undue attention, the riders split up, with two riders in one group and three in the other, each taking a separate route to the rendezvous spot south of Northfield.

After getting settled in south of Northfield, Jesse sent out Frank and Clell to St. Peter and Jim and Billy to Red Wing to check the towns out once again as possible fallback targets. While they were checking on the surrounding towns, the plan was to stake out Northfield for a day to make doubly sure the gang wouldn't run into another armed camp. What Jesse had found in Mankato had him spooked more than a little. He started to think the gang might be better off aborting the whole damn plan and high-tailing it back to Missouri. Jesse hadn't experienced such an eerie feeling of foreboding since his old guerilla commander Bloody-Bill Anderson was killed in an ambush during the war. Though he shook off these unwelcome feelings, he no longer held an unwavering confidence in the success of the gang's Minnesota foray. Creeping doubt was an alien state of mind for a man who had never suffered from a lack of self-righteousness, absolute certainty, and abundant self-confidence. For the first time in his life, Jesse James found himself doubting his decisions and staring at a fate and an outcome he could no longer see clearly.

The next thing Bill remembered was waking up in the local infirmary two days later. Frantic to learn about the confrontation with the bank robbers, Bill asked the nurse to call for the sheriff. An hour later, Sheriff Bob Butts strolled into his room.

"Good to see you up. You know it's been two days since Doc dug that bullet out. Today is September 6," Butts said, shaking his head. "Catching that bullet and being chased to hell and gone by desperadoes must've taken a lot out of ya," Butts added, a broad smile etched into his rugged face.

"Two days. A lot can happen in two days. What about the robbery?" Bill said, desperate to know if they had caught or killed Cole Younger.

"Nothing yet, several folks saw unknown riders near here on both ends of town the morning you came in, but nothing since. We're still keeping a sharp eye out," Butts shared. "Nothing has happened in Northfield or in any of the towns around here, though they've all been warned to double up security. Everyone believes this thing will go down somewhere around here and real soon," Butts continued. "Those outlaws can't sneak around these parts forever. They're going to have to strike or skedaddle soon," he finished.

"I'd like to get back home. My wife must be worried sick. I've been gone three days and she has no idea where I am," Bill said, making a move to get out of bed.

"No need to worry about that. We've asked Sheriff Tillerson down there in Webster County to let your wife know your whereabouts and that you're fine and will be coming home soon," Butts said, motioning for Bill to stay in bed.

After a few minutes the sheriff left to rejoin the vigil. Bill was relieved to know Lucy would be informed of his whereabouts and that she wouldn't be left to worry needlessly. Not knowing for sure why the gang had decided not to hit Mankato, Bill knew he needed to find out, and if necessary, get to Northfield as quickly as possible.

September 6, 1876

Northfield, Rice County, Minnesota

Word to the Wise

BILL WORKED ALL MORNING to convince everybody including Sheriff Butts that he needed to get back home. Though Doc Masters was concerned the wound in his shoulder might reopen from a long ride, he could see no problem in Bill riding back to Lizard Creek if he took it slow. The sheriff was especially grateful to Bill for riding all the way to Mankato to give them a warning. He said he would look Bill up when he got down to Fort Dodge in the fall. It seemed Sheriff Butts was planning to join some friends to do some duck hunting near Fort Dodge in early October. After saying his farewells, Bill was soon on his way.

Bill rode out of town headed south, but soon turned east. Worried he might run into the James-Younger Gang somewhere south of Northfield, he swung around to the northeast and rode into La Sueur County so he could enter Northfield located next door in Rice County from the west. It was a roundabout way, but he suspected that the James-Younger Gang—if they were still in the area—would hole up in Waseca County just south of Northfield. The last thing he needed was another unexpected run-in with Cole Younger.

His plan was to tell the sheriff in Northfield to keep his deputies completely out of sight. The sheriff would need to make everything seem as natural as possible so that when the gang staked out the town, they would see nothing amiss. Mankato had unfortunately looked like an armed camp. It was no wonder Jesse, a trained guerilla fighter, might have become skittish once he got a close look at the welcoming party the town had gathered for him. With all the extra guards and deputies crammed into every doorway and hanging out of every window and loft, an amateur would have had no problem seeing the town was set up for an ambush. If they had really wanted to catch the James-Younger Gang, not just chase them off, they should have hidden their claws and baited the trap.

After seeing what Mankato had done to prepare for the James-Younger Gang, Bill had a plan that he was certain would work. He just needed someone in Northfield to listen to him before the James-Younger Gang gave up and moved on. If they moved on, Bill knew what the outcome would mean for him and Lucy. It would be the end to everything they had built together. He had to take down Cole Younger in Northfield, and God willing, the whole James-Younger Gang. Indeed, success in Northfield was the only chance the Barton family had of surviving together.

He reached Northfield late evening with his shoulder once again throbbing with pain. To numb things a bit, he decided to have a drink or two at a local saloon before looking up the sheriff. He also needed time to figure out how he was going to explain the reason why it was so important for him to come north to Northfield after departing Mankato, rather than returning south to Iowa to his home and his expectant wife and young son and daughter. Northfield and all the towns in southern Minnesota were already prepared for a possible bank robbery. Why should Bill Barton, a mild-mannered farmer from Iowa, need to become any further involved? Bill was having a tough time figuring out how he might spin his story to cover these kinds of questions.

Stepping into the Bull Moose Saloon, he took a stool at the bar with a clear view of the bat-winged doors at the front of the saloon, his favorite spot. The bartender, Teddy, was a man with a perpetual smile and quick wit. His friendly and talkative personality naturally drew customers into a banter that tended to draw out personal information some may have otherwise wished to keep confidential. Bill began to eavesdrop on Teddy's interactions with the customers bellied up to the bar to see if he might be able to find out who was who and what was what.

"So, you're back again tonight, Mac. You look like you've been dancing around in a corset all day," Teddy poked as he grabbed a bottle of blackberry schnapps and looked over his shoulder. "That was a double muleskinner with fresh blackberries on ice, right?" he added.

"Yeah, right. No, I had the chance today to dance with a lamp post on the corner of Fifth and Main. If she was wearin' a corset, it hadn't done a damn thing for her figure, I can tell ya," Mac retorted with a sullen smile. Teddy chuckled, pushing the double muleskinner over in front of Mac. Mac picked up the drink and downed it in a couple of big gulps.

"Try making that a triple, Teddy," Mac said, smacking his lips to savor the sweet flavor of the blackberry schnapps. "If you reuse the fresh blackberries, do I get a discount?" he asked, pushing his empty glass with its fresh blackberries resting on a pile of chiseled ice back toward the bartender with his eyebrows arched upward at a sharp angle.

Sweeping up Mac's glass, Teddy quickly went to work. "A triple muleskinner on the rocks with slightly bruised blackberries, coming up. I'll only charge ya for a double this time. How's that sound, Mac?" Teddy said without missing a beat.

"Sounds like a hell of a bargain," Mac said cheerfully, his mood considerably brighter.

"How long do ya have to continue the stake out?" Teddy inquired as though he were talking about the weather.

"Not sure. I'm not even sure there is anything to stake out. All I know is the extra pay is great and I don't have to put up with my nagging wife every night when I'm on the road," Mac said, chuckling at the thought. Teddy joined in with his own chuckle as he slid the triple muleskinner over in front of Mac.

The two men continued their banter with Mac growing jollier by the drink. Mac no doubt was part of the extra security force that had been brought in to guard the bank. Like Mankato, Northfield was making the same mistakes. They had much of their security personnel visible and posted out on the streets. Bill needed to get to somebody in charge and fast. He had a feeling the James-Younger Gang might strike as soon as the next day.

Bill headed for the sheriff's office, not sure how he would be able to explain his coming to Northfield. On the way, he recognized a face out of the past: Jack Philips, the Pinkerton agent he had tipped off about Billy Chadwell nine years earlier back in Jackson County, Missouri. Jack was the last person he had expected to ever see again. Finding Jack Philips in Northfield just when he needed a way to share his plan to catch Cole Younger was the kind of serendipity that tended to make the world go around these days, Bill thought. Bill had become a true believer in the power of serendipity as it seemed every day he was hearing or reading about one wonderful new discovery or invention after another that had come about by complete accident, discoveries that happened when someone was looking for one thing and ended up finding another even more wonderous thing without expecting it. The recent discovery of the telephone was one such discovery.

According to what Bill had heard, a fella named Alexander Graham Bell, while trying to make a better telegraph or some such, discovered by accident how to send voices over the same wires. According to the newspapers, the demonstration of this unbelievable discovery in June at the Philadelphia Centennial Exposition had been a smashing success. For Bill, such a wonderous thing was difficult to even fathom. That men could now talk directly to one another through copper wires at great distance was nothing short of a miracle. He struggled to imagine all the ways Bell's discovery would change the world. That such a history-altering discovery had come about by pure accident was even more difficult to understand.

Though he might not be able to understand the depth of wonder of such discoveries, he could understand that stumbling onto Jack Philips here in Northfield, at the very moment he needed a way to share his plan to catch the James-Younger Gang, was a stroke of luck more wonderous than anything he could ever have hoped to discover in his lifetime. Bill would have pinched himself to make sure he wasn't dreaming had his shoulder not already been crying out in pain. He decided right then and there to approach Jack as the recently resurrected Leroy Thompson. Since it seemed the original tip Leroy gave to Jack nine years ago finally paid off, Jack might even be happy to see Leroy again. Bill was certain that ol' Billy Chadwell was definitely one of the riders he had seen come up behind Charlie Pitts on that fateful night back at Lizard Creek just three days ago. He now suspected that was why Jack was here.

Bill followed Jack for two blocks until Jack swiveled around without warning, his pistol drawn and pointed directly at Bill's chest. "You have business with me, mister?" Jack growled, his face hard and mean.

"Whoa now, Jack, it's me, Leroy, Leroy Thompson. I thought I recognized you and wanted to buy you a drink," Bill said as calmly as possible, keeping his right hand clear of his pistol and avoiding any sudden moves.

"Well, I'll be damned. Is that you, Leroy? You are a sight for sore eyes. Damn man, I guess we've all aged a little. It's been nearly ten years since I last saw you," Jack said sliding his pistol back into its holster. "Sorry about drawing on you like that, but Pinkerton men have been getting shot in the back a lot in recent years. When you kept following without saying anything, I got spooked," Jack admitted apologetically.

"No problem. These are dangerous times. Speaking of which I'd like to talk to you about why you're here," Bill said, looking directly at Jack.

Jack stared back at Bill, seeming to size him up while putting two and two together.

"I imagine you guessed we're following the tip you provided back in Missouri," Jack said. "It was simple enough, stake out and follow ol' Billy, if he moves north, we might have a chance to finally track down the James-Younger Gang. We did just that. We're now convinced this thing is going down here in Northfield tomorrow. We received a confirmation just a little over two days ago that Northfield is on the gang's short list," Jack shared, lowering his voice.

"Did that additional information come from Mankato?" Bill asked, knowing Jack would be surprised Leroy knew such a detail.

"How do you know that? Never mind. What's this all about, Leroy? Why are you here?" Jack said, wanting to know why Leroy Thompson had suddenly popped up in Northfield, Minnesota after all these years just as the James-Younger Gang was rumored to be preparing to rob the local bank.

"We need to talk. Follow me. Let's get a drink," Bill said as he motioned for Jack to follow him. "I need a little numb juice, my shoulder is killin' me," Bill added as he pointed to his blood-stained shirt and led the way down a side street, where he spotted a little place called the Royal Stallion Bar & Grill.

As the men entered, the first thing they noticed was that the place was nearly empty. It didn't take them long to understand why. The cliental visiting this fine establishment all headed straight upstairs where fine upstanding scantily-clad ladies ushered them into private rooms.

"Just take the stairway to heaven, gentlemen. Suzy at the top of the stairs will see to it that your needs are well taken care of," the bartender said without looking up as he continued polishing a row of shot glasses.

"Just a couple whiskeys. Make' em doubles. We'll take the table in the corner," Bill said, leading Jack to a table in the back corner facing the door.

Soon after they sat down, a thin, tired-looking barmaid, sporting a freshly minted shiner which had nearly closed her right eye shut, shuffled over to their table in a see-through nightgown that left little to the imagination. Without a word or so much as a smile, she placed their drinks on the table and shuffled back behind the bar, her bare buttocks covered in cuts and bruises.

"Gentlemen, just give a yell when you need a refill or when you decide to sample our services upstairs," the bartender hollered without much enthusiasm before returning to his polishing.

"Sorry about the choice of bars. At least we have the place to ourselves," Bill said, sickened by the obvious mistreatment of the women working at the ever-popular Royal Stallion.

Bill told Jack a story very similar to the one he had told Sheriff Bob Butts in Mankato. In his new version of the story, he was Leroy Thompson on business in northern Iowa when he had been waylaid by the James-Younger Gang and shot getting away. During the ensuing chase, he had overheard the gang's plan to hit either Mankato or Northfield. Seeing Billy Chadwell riding with the James-Younger Gang this far north had confirmed for him they were finally planning to pull off the job they had talked about so long ago in Missouri. With all of Sheriff Butts' extra security so visibly stationed around the town in Mankato, it was no surprise the gang might have chosen to avoid such an obvious ambush.

The reason he had come to Northfield was to tell the local sheriff to take his men off the streets and to try to make the town appear as peaceful and normal as possible. No guns, no men on the streets, no undue attention to the bank, nothing to give an outsider any clue the set-up was a trap. Men should be ready with guns cocked, all should be well-hidden, none in plain view. He went on to outline how the town should bait the trap. He assured Jack that if the gang staked out the town and found that everything looked harmless and peaceful, they wouldn't be able to resist taking down the bank. The bait would make things even more inviting.

Jack agreed the plan was good and understood that the towns in the area had been doing what law enforcement always does, making their deterrents visible to prevent crime, rather than setting a trap to catch desperadoes. The towns were trying to shoo the flies away, rather than inviting them to land so they could be smashed. Jack said he would take care of it from here and that Leroy Thompson should make himself scarce, since the gang all knew what he looked like. The two men continued to talk for some time about life and the future and how a person never quite knew what might come next. Bill found he liked Jack and he thought Jack might feel the same about him. Their easy ways tended to mesh well, their conversation flowed naturally. Bill was sorry they had never been friends.

When the men parted company, Bill was relieved to have found a way to put his plan into action. Jack would spread the word and make sure the town was ready by tomorrow morning. Jack made Leroy promise that he wouldn't go to the sheriff with his story. Jack was adamant that he would take care of things and that Leroy wasn't to share his story or his plan with anyone else. Jack also made Leroy promise that if he was ever asked, he would say he had never known a Jack Philips and had never heard of him or met him in either Missouri or Minnesota. Bill considered Jack's request and on reflection he could clearly see why the Pinkertons would want to have their part in the operation hidden from public knowledge. If the James-Younger Gang went down, the Pinkertons wanted it to appear that they had played no part in it. Having been an intelligence officer himself, he understood many things happened through the actions of faceless people working behind the scenes that history would never record.

Leroy Thompson had lived and died and had been resurrected. Now that he had put everything in Jack's hands, the time had come for Leroy to die once more. Bill hoped this time Leroy would stay dead and buried once and for all. Parting Jack's company, Bill headed up the boardwalk in search of a hotel with a hot bath and a good bed, one without any extra Royal Stallion services.

Looking down a dark alley on his way to Main Street, he witnessed a bobtail tomcat pounce on a large mouse coming out from under a stack of crates. He watched as the tomcat sank his canines into his prey's throat. Holding the squirming mouse by its neck, the tomcat pranced off up the alley and was soon swallowed by the night. Bill knew this was an ominous sign that couldn't be ignored. Its meaning seemed clear enough. He just wondered in his cat and mouse game with Cole Younger who would end up playing the role of the cat and who the role of the mouse.

September 7, 1876

Northfield, Rice County, Minnesota

Western Waterloo

JESSE WAS UP EARLY. Both sets of riders, Frank and Billy, and Jim and Clell, had returned the day before and reported that both Red Wing and St. Peter had armed security on the streets. Jesse didn't like the sound of their reports one iota. First Mankato and now other towns in the area, all with armed security on the streets. It didn't seem right somehow. Things had gotten tougher in recent years, Jesse would be the first to admit; however, he wondered why folks in these parts where so damn worried about crime. It might just be a sign of the times, Cole had told him. Jesse decided they would scout out Northfield one last time and if things didn't look right, they would abort their foray into Minnesota and head back to Missouri, where the banks might not be as juicy, but were a damn sight less risky.

Jesse, Cole, and Bobby would enter Northfield from the south. Using back streets, Jesse and Cole would check out both ends of Main Street. Bobby would once again take a ten-dollar bill to the bank to make change. This should allow the three of them to get a good feel for the whole setup from inside and outside the bank and from both ends of town. The men split up with a plan to meet back at the same spot behind one of the town's outer horse stables in an hour.

When Cole and Jesse came back from their survey of both ends of town, Bobby was waiting for them with a small white bag in his hand and chewing on a piece of saltwater taffy.

"What in the hell. Where did you get this?" Cole said as he grabbed the bag out of Bobby's hand.

Startled by Cole's reaction, Bobby's face turned beet red. "I stopped at the General Store to get a little something to chew on. No big deal, it's all quiet at the bank and inside the store across the street," Bobby said, grabbing back the bag and squaring his shoulders.

"Cole's just worried you might accidentally do something to set off an alarm. Checking inside the store across the street from the bank was a good move," Jesse said, quickly cutting in. "We're all just wantin' things to go smoothly," he added, hoping to soothe the Younger brothers and pleased to find out Bobby had a sweet tooth.

Knowing the store across the street from the bank didn't have any armed security watching the bank was comforting news. Jesse had watched several shops along Main Street send deposits to the bank that morning. He was sure the town was ripe and ready for picking.

"Yeah, good job, Bobby. Sorry to snap at ya. You're my little brother and I just want everything to go without a hitch. Goin' into the store to see if it was clean was a good move," Cole said as he patted Bobby on the shoulder. "Now, how about a piece of that saltwater taffy?" Cole added.

"Me too," Jesse chimed in as both outlaws held out their rough calloused hands like a couple of little kids on Christmas morning.

Bobby handed them each a couple pieces of taffy and put another one in his mouth. The outlaws followed suit and all three mounted up and rode out, chewing on saltwater taffy. The taffy was mouth-watering, and they all believed the loot in the bank would be just as juicy.

Bill, taking Jack's advice, decided to spend the day inside his hotel room out of sight. The hotel being on the same side of the street as the bank prevented him from directly seeing the front of the bank. To solve this problem, he had chosen a room with a view of the General Store opposite the bank. By using a pair of binoculars, he was able to clearly see the bank's reflection in the large plate glass windows of the General Store.

All morning, Bill couldn't help checking the front of the bank in the General Store's windows. Bill even decided to take his meals in his room. After quickly wolfing down a light lunch, he sat back from the window to stay out of view from the street as he sipped coffee and looked out at the boardwalk opposite the hotel through a slit in the lace curtains. It didn't take Bill a second to recognize Bobby Younger ambling up the boardwalk and then cutting across the street toward the bank. Bill noted that Bobby was unarmed. It was clear the gang was casing the town and that Bobby had been sent to check out the inside of the bank. Bill could only hope that Jack had ensured everyone was acting naturally and that any armed men were well out of sight. Bill was now convinced that the James-Younger Gang would strike within the hour if they sensed there was no threat. If the gang got spooked off this time, Bill knew he would have a vengeful Cole Younger on the loose gunning for him sooner rather than later.

Bill had asked Jack to have a few shop owners pretend to carry their deposits to the bank throughout the day. Bill wanted any gang members who might be scouting the town to get the impression the bank was a fat juicy one and ripe for the picking. Throughout the morning, Bill had noticed deposit bags being carried to the bank from several shops. He was sure if anyone was staking out the town, they would have seen at least one or two of these trips to the bank.

Leaving the bank, Bobby crossed the street and went directly into the General Store. After a few moments, Bobby left the General Store and headed back up the boardwalk carrying a small white paper bag. Bill couldn't help but worry whether the armed men stationed in the store had been out of sight when Bobby unexpectedly came in from the street. He knew everyone would know the answer to that question within an hour, one way or the other.

As the afternoon dragged on, things remained quiet on Main Street. It had been more than an hour since Bobby's visit to the bank and the General Store, and Bill could feel a hidden tension struggling to keep itself from bursting into the streets. It seemed possible that Bobby might have seen something he didn't like while in the store. Just when he thought all his running around had been in vain, Bill heard the jingle of tack and spurs before he saw three riders wearing long dusters slowly make their way up the street. Using his binoculars to get a closer look at the reflection in the store windows, he could clearly see Frank and Jesse James and Bobby Younger tie up their horses and head into the bank. Bill also noticed Bobby Younger and Frank James pull rifles from their scabbards and slip them under their long dusters before entering the bank.

Only a few minutes passed before five more riders came up in front of the bank. Three riders got off their horses and took up positions on each side of the bank's front door. The other two riders stayed mounted, each looking toward opposite ends of Main Street. It didn't surprise Bill that Billy Chadwell was one of the mounted riders considering his bum leg. Bill had no trouble identifing the other rider as Clell Miller: his appearance was unmistakable, with his long red hair hanging down from under his gentleman's Derby and his sanguine complexion standing in stark contrast to his trademark shiny white pearl-handled pistols. Bill knew, like Billy Chadwell, Clell Miller was an outlaw who was known to ride with the James-Younger Gang as an extra gun hand. Unlike Billy Chadwell, Clell Miller was more than just an extra gun hand, he was a notorious gunslinger with a growing reputation. The moment ol' Billy Chadwell pulled out his pistol, a cry out of nowhere echoed down the street: "He's got a gun, they're robbing the bank!" As if on cue, gunfire erupted from every direction.

Inside the bank, Frank and Bobby held their rifles on a small group of hostages made up of bank staff and customers who had been forced into a back corner of the lobby, a tactic used by the gang many times in the past. Jesse held the bank manager at gunpoint and demanded he open the vault. The manger resisted and claimed the vault couldn't be opened and that it was on an automatic timer of some sort. Jesse was hearing none of it.

"Open the goddamn vault or die, your choice," Jesse said forcefully with what sounded like the voice of a demon straight out of hell, causing several of the hostages to audibly groan in fear. The tension in the room was growing by the second, as the standoff between Jesse and the bank manager sped towards an increasingly unavoidable fatal conclusion.

In this surreal moment between life and death, the attention of everyone inside the bank shifted to a muffled cry that rang out from somewhere outside in the street. The melee that followed in the next few seconds at first baffled both the outlaws and hostages inside the bank. As if a sudden hailstorm had swept over the town, the popping and cracking of gunfire seemed to break out from all directions. Windows shattered and boards splintered as a torrent of lead smashed into the front of the bank.

As gunfire rang out and bullets rained down from every direction, Bill saw everything at the front of the bank and for some distance on either side suddenly riddled with holes as glass shards and wood splinters flew. It was obvious the armed men, while trying to stay undercover, were firing their weapons indiscriminately in the general direction of the bank without taking aim at anything in particular. Even so, the mounted riders made easy targets. Both riders caught by the first volley of hot lead were killed instantly. Bill could see Billy Chadwell catch four slugs directly in his chest as blood exploded from the wounds, his horse taking multiple hits was also brought down kicking and screaming. Billy's lifeless body fell motionless in a bloody heap as his horse continued to flail and snort as it lay bleeding in the middle of the street.

Clell Miller's horse had reared up at the first crack of gunfire, exposing its belly to the full violence of the first volley. Holes sprouted across the horse's torso, ripping the animal apart as guts and blood flew in every direction. Miller, unable to draw a pistol while fighting to get control of his horse, took multiple hits, one taking off the top of his head, sending his Derby rimmed in red hair flying off down the street. As limp as a ragdoll, his decapitated and riddled body laid crushed under the shredded carcass of his toppled horse. His shiny white pearl-handled pistols still in their holsters rested oddly untouched and out of place amid all the blood and the gore. Gun smoke hung thick in the air as the battle continued to rage.

Cole and his brother Jim had taken cover behind the porch posts on each side of the bank's front door while Charlie Pitts huddled just inside the open door of the bank and motioned for the James brothers and Bobby Younger to get a move on. Bill, not wanting to let the outlaws get away, decided he would try to get a few shots off when they mounted up to make a run for it. Cole and Jim, both with guns drawn and firing in every direction, mounted their horses and readied the other horses for a quick getaway.

"Times up, open the vault right now or I'll kill ya where ya stand. Don't dare doubt me," Jesse said though clenched teeth, his tone deadly.

"I couldn't do it even if I wanted, the timer . . . ," the manager said, his words becoming the last ones he would ever utter. Without batting an eye, Jesse emptied his pistol in the manager's chest. At close range, each bullet hammered the man's body backward with every impact until he was finally pushed up against the wall, where he slid down into a seated position with his legs outstretched in a wide vee in front of him. Gun smoke hung in the air above the manager's dead body, his chest a bloody ruin, an expression of surprise and disbelief frozen on his face. With that, Jesse, Frank, and Bobby made their way to the front door.

Shots continued to sporadically ring out. However, now that the gang was returning fire in every direction, the number of townsfolk and deputies brave enough to fire while being shot at had grown scant, to say the least. The angle of Bill's hotel room window only afforded him a shot at the gang when they were in the middle of the street or directly in front of the General Store opposite the bank. The outlaws mounted their horses while Cole, Jim, and Charlie Pitts provided cover fire. As they turned to ride out of town, for a brief instant, Bill had a clear shot from his hotel room window. He fired twice and was sure one of his shots hit Cole in the left leg when he saw blood fly up where Cole grabbed at his thigh just as he rode out of Bill's line of sight.

The frightened hostages in the bank had huddled in terror behind the teller windows as the gun battle raged at the front of the bank. Susan Wilson cried uncontrollably as she looked over at Joe Heywood, the bank manager, who now sat upright on the floor with his back against the wall as blood pooled around him from the multiple gunshot wounds that had shredded his chest. His eyes, wide open, stared at her, though they had long since ceased seeing anything in the world of the living. Susan just couldn't understand why he had refused to open the vault or why the outlaws themselves hadn't tried the vault's door handle. With so many shopkeepers bringing in deposits since early morning, the vault door had been unlocked all day.

As quickly as it had started, it was over. Men ran into the street, several firing at the fleeing outlaws. Bill rushed downstairs and saw that several people had been wounded, mostly from flying glass, with one innocent man dead from a gunshot wound to the head, and several others laying wounded along the boardwalk. The two dead outlaws were getting a lot of attention from a gawking crowd that had gathered in the middle of the street. The wounded horse laid on its side, snorting and crying out in pain, its legs twitching in uncontrollable spasms. Men carrying rifles and pistols poured into the street as the sheriff began to shout out the names of the men who would be riding with the posse. The sheriff then, without ceremony, walked over with pistol in hand and finished off the wounded horse with a single shot to its brain.

When Jack came into the street, he saw Bill standing in front of the hotel and walked over. Jack said he would be riding with the posse that was already getting saddled up and would be going after the desperadoes in a few minutes. He assured Bill that with at least three of the gang members wounded and several of their horses shot up, they wouldn't get far. Jack was determined to see the job through to the bitter end.

He wished Leroy luck, and thanked him for all his help in finally tracking down the James-Younger Gang and in hopefully bringing them to justice. He also wished Leroy a happy wedding, having learned Leroy would be getting married soon. During their conversation at the Royal Stallion, Jack had shared personal details of his life. For one, Jack planned to put in for a desk job at the Pinkerton National Detective Agency headquarters in Chicago as soon as the James-Younger Gang business was settled. Jack also shared that he was through with fieldwork and tracking down desperadoes. He had gotten married a year ago and wanted to get started on a family. He felt fieldwork was just too damn dangerous for a man with small children. He also admitted he was afraid he was losing his edge.

Bill shared some of his personal details as well, at least the Leroy Thompson version of his life. Bill had told Jack he too would be getting married soon and that his days as a vagabond were over. Bill didn't share where exactly he would settle down or that he already had two children and was expecting a third child soon from the woman he planned to marry. Though he wanted to share more with the man he had come to like and that he felt was a friend, Bill knew that for Jack Philips, the memory of Leroy Thompson needed to remain that he was a southerner, a drifter, a single man, and a man without roots.

"You be careful. Wouldn't want your new wife to become a widow before you two have the chance to make all those babies you're planning on. I might swing by Chicago to see ya someday," Bill said as a final farewell.

"You do that, Leroy. Take care of yourself. No reason to hang around here to see how things turn out, you can read all about it in the newspapers. I'm not sure how you swindled a woman into marrying you or how she'll ever put up with you, but I truly wish you all the best," Jack said, truly meaning every word.

The two men shook hands like long-lost brothers. They then looked at each other for a beat until both men nodded. Jack turned, pulled his hat down tight on his head, and hustled up the street to join the posse. Bill watched the posse ride out and went back to his room to gather up his things. Though it was already getting late in the afternoon, he soon checked out and started the long ride back to Lizard Creek.

As he rode out of Northfield, he agreed with Jack. There was no need to stay around when he could read about how things turned out in the newspapers. He also knew he needed to get back to Lizard Creek to prepare for two possible outcomes. The first was if Cole escaped and became free to roam again. The second was if Cole was killed or captured. Bill and Lucy now stood at a fork in the road that would define their future together and that of their children. Which branch they would travel, only the wind knew.

With that thought on his mind, Bill sought for a sign to help point the way, but found none, other than the faint cooing of turtle doves and the deep blue bowl of a cloudless sky. Bill clung to the hope that these scant signs seemed to portend that he and Lucy might finally find the peace they had sought for so long.

September 10, 1876

Lizard Creek, Webster County, Iowa

Home Sweet Home

WITH THE PAIN IN his shoulder increasing by the mile, Bill was exhausted when he arrived back at his farm on Lizard Creek after more than two days on the trail. Lucy, her belly as large as an October pumpkin, bounded out of the house to meet him as he rounded the last fencepost on the gate to the yard. Johnny and little Alda came running around the house from the backyard, waving their arms. Lucy and the kids couldn't wait to hug him tightly as soon as he got down off his horse. All he could think of was how good it was to finally be home. He had been gone only a week, but it seemed like a lifetime.

He had stopped in Fort Dodge for a few hours to rest up and to buy a few presents before riding on into Lizard Creek. He picked up candy, glass marbles, and ribbons for Johnny and Alda, some floral scented soap for Lucy, and a new baby blanket for the little one on the way. With on-again off-again rain showers blowing through, Bill had all his purchases wrapped up in thick waxed paper to keep everything dry. The packages of numerous sizes had been tied onto his back saddle conchos and to his saddlebags on both sides. When little Alda first saw him and took everything in, she said that her pa looked like an old traveling peddler with all his bundles of goods hanging down on both sides of his horse. Her innocent remark caused everyone to laugh with abandon.

After stepping down from his horse, Bill was swarmed with hugs and kisses. It was, without question, great to be home again. Once things settled down, Bill set out to loosen the tiedowns on the many packages. Everyone was excited to see what he had brought.

"Did you bring the cookies?" Alda asked, watching him closely. Bill suddenly remembered he had put Charlotte's cookies in his right saddlebag and hadn't checked on them or taken them out since he left Rockwell City. Reaching into the saddlebag, Bill came out with a wad of paper soaked through here and there with oily patches. Bill realized the cookies had been smashed flatter than a pancake when he had laid his horse down on its side to hide in the tall grass during his escape from the Youngers. For the past seven days, the cookies had remained wedged into the seams of his right saddlebag, growing staler and oilier by the day.

"Well, Princess, I'm afraid they got smushed up a little," Bill said, holding up the oily mangled package of cookies with a sad frown on his face.

With furrowed brow and narrowed eyelids, Alda stood silent for a moment, her hands on her hips looking back and forth between her pa's face masked in misery and the mangled package of cookies. She then reached out and took the package from her pa's hand. "Don't be so sad, pa, my pet goat Andy is gonna love 'em!" she said with enthusiasm and then hugged her pa with all her might, and though he had to wince a little as his shoulder was still raw, he hugged her back just as hard. With that everyone once again laughed with abandon.

In the following days, Bill was back to tending his farm. His corn needed to be harvested and he had a list of repairs and chores that needed to be taken care of before the weather turn colder. Wilber had looked in on the place in his absence and had done what he could. With his own place to take care of and ten kids to chase after, there were real limits on how much time Wilber could spend working Bill's place. Bill appreciated the fact that Wilber was always there and ready to pitch in. Bill had grown to believe that it had taken strong families to hone a new nation out of the wilderness and that it would take strong families to tame the lands further west. His dream was to have his sons and daughters be part of that adventure.

Day by day, Bill and Lucy waited for word. After a week had passed, the news from Fort Dodge was that the James-Younger Gang was still on the run. There had been reports of sightings of the gang, yet all the desperadoes remained on the loose. Learning that the gang might head south, Bill worried the men would try to take the same path home that they used to ride north to Minnesota. If they did, they would be headed straight for Lizard Creek.

He wondered how much longer they would have to wait. He knew Cole, Bobby, and Jim had all been wounded and he was sure several of their horses had taken lead. He wasn't sure about Jesse, Frank, or Charlie, though he was sure their horses had also been wounded. He couldn't understand how the gang had been able to outfox the massive manhunt he knew was underway. Every town in the area had beefed up its security in anticipation of a possible bank robbery. Many of those men were now taking part in the statewide manhunt.

Bill had never wanted to know the outcome of anything more in his life than the fate of Cole Younger. He knew, one way or another, he would learn Cole's fate and his own. It was just a matter of time. Even so, every evening he looked to the natural rhythms of things around him and searched the sky for an omen but found nothing to reassure his restless mind, only horsetail clouds dancing high in the heavens marking the change of seasons. As a natural sign, horsetail clouds, Bill had been taught long ago, pointed only to the uncertainty of events yet to unfold or yet to be determined.

September 21, 1876

Madelia, Watonwa County, Minnesota

End of the Line

AFTER FINALLY GIVING THE relentless Northfield posse the slip, the gang gathered south of Mankato at their original rendezvous spot on the Blue Earth River. They had been on the run for a week and hadn't been able to get out of the state. Frequent rain showers had aided in repeatedly washing the gang's tracks out, but the posse refused to give up the hunt. Jesse and Frank had stolen fresh horses and wanted to make a run for it southwest into the Dakota Territory. The Youngers with Bobby badly wounded in the arm, Jim with shoulder wounds, and Cole with several wounds including a bullet lodged in his left leg, wanted to find a place to hole up. Hoping to fool the relentless manhunt, the gang decided to split up, with Charlie Pitts and the Youngers heading straight west to find a good place to hide out and the James brothers, now on fresh horses, riding straight south before turning west towards the Dakota Territory. The idea behind the plan was that the posse would follow the James brothers, believing the gang was headed south straight back to Missouri. Everyone was convinced this maneuver would allow the gang to escape the hangman's noose.

Due to the frequent rains, the rivers in the area had swollen greatly, making river crossing difficult. The Youngers' horses, wounded during the gun battle, soon gave out from exhaustion. Having no other choice, they decided they might be able to make better time on foot. After nearly a week of zigging and zagging across unfamiliar countryside, they came upon a remote place in the woods in Watonwa County near Madelia that provided good cover where they thought they would be able to get patched up and have time to plot their next moves. They had no more than gotten settled into their makeshift shelter when their hideaway was stumbled upon by local hunters. They soon found themselves face to face with the local sheriff and a posse of armed men.

"Goddamn it Charlie, how many are there?" Cole barked when Charlie ducked back into the makeshift-shelter they had fixed up to stay out of the rain.

"Looks like six or seven. Problem is, I heard 'em call out that others were on the way," Charlie sadly reported. "Doesn't look good, Cole. How do we play it?" he added, looking at Cole letting him know the decision was his.

Knowing they had no horses to flee on, and that even if they did, they were in no condition to do so anyway, Cole with a blood-soaked bandage on his left leg looked over his troops. He looked first at Jim, who had two slugs in his right shoulder, and then at Bobby, his right arm nearly blown off at the elbow, the wound still bleeding badly, and finally at Charlie, who had miraculously avoided all the flying lead. Cole then stood up and squared his shoulders as best he could and said with a snarl, "We hit the bastards head on, if'n you're all with me."

"Capitan, we were with ya when we started, and we'll be with ya to the end," Charlie replied, dead serious and without hesitation. Bobby and Jim nodded their agreement.

"Alright then, let's get ready to kill some of these blue-bellied sons-of-bitches," Cole said as he checked the loads in his pistols. Following his lead, the other men took to loading their weapons.

Before long, the gang heard Sheriff Jim Gliptin yell out, "Come out with your hands in the air, we have you surrounded." Just as Cole readied himself to reply, another voice yelled out, "There they are, they have guns, shoot!" With that, gunfire erupted from all sides.

Amid the pitched gun battle, Charlie Pitts charged out from behind the makeshift-shelter at a full run with pistols blazing in both hands. Horses had been tied up nearby and it seemed Charlie had decided to make a break for one of them. Charlie got less than ten paces before his body was riddled with gunshots. Dead before hitting the ground, he fell with a wild look in his piggy bloodshot eyes, his pistols still blazing. The Youngers fought on, all taking additional wounds until finally running out of ammunition. Waving a bloody white flag, Cole Younger and his brothers, all bleeding from multiple gunshot wounds, surrendered.

Nearly a hundred men surrounding their makeshift-shelter on all sides had eventually joined in on the final turkey shoot. The outlaws never had a chance. The Youngers were soon handcuffed and taken into custody. After their wounds had been looked over by a doctor on the scene, the sheriff called for a wagon to be brought in to take the prisoners back to jail in Faribault in Rice County to stand trial for murder. As the hubbub calmed down and the crowd thinned out, Jack Philips, who had helped track the outlaws for nearly two weeks, made his way over to where the Younger brothers sat in a row on a pile of freshly-cut logs.

"Just came over to say hello," Jack said to Cole with a broad smile.

"Go to hell," Cole said not certain how he would get out of the current situation and not needing any further insult.

"Yeah, I'll leave you alone soon enough. I wanted to say hello from the Pinkys and from Leroy Thompson," Jack said flatly, looking down at Cole still sporting a smile.

"Hell, I suspected you were a Pinky when you were working back in Jackson County. I should've kilt ya then. What's this about Leroy?" Cole shot back, meeting Jack eye to eye.

"Oh, not much. Leroy just asked me to send his regards and to deliver a message," Jack said shrugging his shoulders and looking squarely at Cole, curious to see his reaction.

"What the hell do the Pinkys have to do with a no-good horse thief like Leroy Thompson? Then again, I guess the bastard works both sides of everything," Cole said, realizing he had once again underestimated Leroy Thompson.

"Now Cole, you hurt my feelings. Leroy's a friend of mine," Jack said, having fun playing with Cole now that he had finally tracked the son-of-a-bitch down and had him right where he wanted him after so many years.

"So, what's the message?" Cole asked, no longer surprised Leroy had a connection with Jack Philips and the Pinkertons or anybody else on both sides of the law.

"He told me if I ever got the chance to talk to you, face to face like, I should say, 'There're only two hearts that'll ever beat as one and neither of 'em will ever be yours.' I'm not sure what he meant, but I promised him I would deliver his message, word for word, so there you have it," Jack said, still meeting Cole's stare eye to eye.

Jack didn't know why Leroy wanted his message delivered word for word. He figured there must be bad blood between the two men that went back a long way. That Cole had tried to kill Leroy on sight confirmed Cole had a grudge against the man. That Leroy had done all he could to assist in Cole's capture confirmed again the grudge ran both ways. Jack had no idea what it might be all about.

Cole's mind raced, wondering how Leroy could possibly know his deepest secret feelings for his Lucy-belle, the love of his life. Feelings he had never had a chance to even share with Lucy-belle and had spoken out loud only once in his life on the day he ordered the jeweler in Kansas City to have those words etched into the band of the diamond wedding ring he still wore next to his heart on a leather strap around his neck. Like a bolt of lightning, Cole suddenly remembered that morning at the Kansas City jewelry shop when a faceless customer had entered the shop and had become by his presence the only other person in the world who had heard him put into words his innermost feelings for Lucy-belle Breeden.

Shaking his head back and forth in disbelief, he reached up and tugged hard on the leather strap around his neck until it snapped. Handing the broken strap with a diamond ring dangling on it to Jack, Cole said in almost a whisper, "Tell Leroy, this is for his bride. I hope their two hearts will beat as one forever."

Jack was momentarily stunned by Cole's sudden and unexpected reaction and by his surprise gift for Leroy's bride. In a kind of surreal awe-filled moment, Jack found himself staring at the wonderous beauty of a dazzling two-carat diamond ring dangling from a loop of leather he now held in his hand. Before he could walk away, Cole reached up and grabbed his arm. Looking down at Cole, Jack witnessed the sudden transformation of Cole's face as it morphed into an evil ghoulish mask. With his eyes ablaze with hatred, Cole growled, "Oh, and be sure to tell the no-good son-of-a-bitch, he may have her now, but I had her first, and more than once."

After Cole uttered his vile and bitter remark, Jack noticed a tear run down the outlaw's dirty blood-stained cheek. Seeing such a blood-thirsty desperado cry was a sight Jack Philips could never have imagined he would ever witness. In disgust, Jack slid the ring off the broken leather strap and put it in his shirt pocket. Without another word, he tossed the strap in the mud, tipped his hat at Cole and his brothers, and while buttoning up his shirt pocket, he walked off, got on his horse, and spurred its flanks.

Tears continued to stream down Cole's cheeks as he watched Jack ride off until he disappeared over the last rolling hill. As Cole sat waiting for the wagon to come that would haul the prisoners back to Rice County, he looked aimlessly at the ground in front of him. As his eyes drifted from one thing to another, they came to focus on the discarded broken leather strap he had worn around his neck for the last ten years. It now lay twisted in the mud in the shape of a heart. A broken heart, he thought. Cole couldn't help but chuckle at the irony of such a coincidence.

In coming days, Cole, Jim, and Bob Younger were tried in the town of Faribault in Rice County, Minnesota where they were found guilty of murder and received 25-year sentences in Stillwater Prison.

Frank and Jesse James somehow miraculously escaped unharmed and made it back to Missouri, where Jesse continued his outlaw ways.

September 23, 1876

Chicago, Cook County, Illinois

Ashes to Ashes

AFTER RIDING TO MANKATO, Jack caught the train to St. Paul and then east on to Chicago, arriving only two days after the Youngers had been captured. Walking into the Pinkerton National Detective Agency headquarters, Jack headed directly to the president's office. When he stepped into the outer office, Miss Anne Johnson, the president's private secretary, still as prim and plump as ever, greeted him with professional courtesy despite his rough-looking attire. Jack hadn't had time to clean up from his more than two-week posse ride across southern Minnesota chasing down the Youngers. His face was unshaven and was covered in heavy stubble. His clothes were wrinkled and covered in sweat and mud stains. His odor was enough to tell anyone within fifty feet that the man was badly in need of a good scrubbing. Even his boots still caked in mud left a trail of earthy crumbs on floors and carpets wherever he trod.

Jack had sent a telegram ahead informing the agency he would be arriving in Chicago today. The reply Jack received by hand-carried courier upon his arrival in Chicago had come directly from Mr. Allan J. Pinkerton himself and had ordered Jack to talk to no one and to come straight to the president's office. He had done just that. Miss Johnson had obviously been expecting him. It was also obvious she had not quite expected him to arrive looking and smelling like an unwashed saddle bum down on his luck.

"This way please, Mr. Philips," Miss Johnson said tipping off her seat and leading the way. After tapping twice on the president's inner office door, she opened it and ushered Mr. Philips through the door.

"Mr. Philips has arrived," she announced curtly. She then nodded at Jack and without further word left the room, leaving Jack facing the president's desk.

Once the door closed, Allan Pinkerton looked up from a thick file he had been reading, one of mountains of files, newspapers, and loose documents that buried his desk, and turned his attention to Jack. On Pinkerton's face was the biggest grin Jack had ever witnessed on any man. "Jack, my boy, so we finally nailed the sons-of-bitches!" he exclaimed as if a great weight had been lifted off his shoulders. There was no denying that the mounting public relations crisis for the agency had been in large part resolved. With the demise of the James-Younger Gang, public interest would quickly wane.

"Please sit down and tell me all about it," he continued, motioning to the large leather upholstered chair positioned in front of his desk.

Jack sat down and didn't really know where to begin. After gathering his thoughts and just as he was about to begin telling his tale, Pinkerton interrupted by raising his right hand and motioning for Jack to just sit tight.

"Sorry about my bad manners. I'm just so excited to learn all the details of your successful operation, I forgot to ask you if you needed a little refreshment. You look like a man in need of a drink," Pinkerton said as he stood up. "How about a fine private label bourbon with branch water? It should help wet your whistle and calm your nerves after your long journey," he added with enthusiasm. Walking over to a cabinet built into the wall, he quickly made two drinks and placed Jack's on a small side table next to his chair.

Settling back into his chair behind his desk, Pinkerton took a sip of his drink, indicated his satisfaction with its quality, and said, "Now, tell me everything from the top. Start with your arrival in Northfield." The reason Pinkerton wanted to hear the story directly from Jack is that he was concerned any written reports might get into the wrong hands. None of the agency's recorded events involving the tracking down of the James-Younger Gang would survive once the case was closed.

With that, Jack downed about half of his bourbon with branch water and began. After he had recounted the events of the last three weeks, Jack finished his whiskey and sat quietly waiting for Pinkerton's reaction. Pinkerton sat motionless, his elbows on his desk with his forearms forming an A-frame, his chin resting atop his cupped hands, his face deep in thought.

"So, let's go over the facts of the case, one more time," Pinkerton said, finally breaking the silence that had ruled the room after Jack finished recounting recent events.

"Leroy Thompson happened to bump into you in Northfield and told you he had been shot by the James-Younger Gang and that he had learned of their plans by overhearing them talking during his getaway. Wounded, he had ridden to Mankato, the gang's primary target. While there he saw how the town deployed their security and felt the sight of so much armed security on the street was the reason the gang may have been spooked off. He then went to Northfield to ensure the same mistake wouldn't be made again. In sum, he tipped us off about Billy Chadwell and how to track down the James-Young Gang. He then narrowed our attention down to two target towns, Mankato and Northfield. After observing how Mankato deployed their armed security, he believed they may have spooked off the gang. He then rode to Northfield with a plan of action that involved the town hiding its claws and baiting the trap, so to speak. In many ways, it could be said that Leroy Thompson was solely responsible for the demise of the notorious James-Younger Gang. To top it off, he seems to have done it all for love. The love of a woman who had been, it appears, Cole Younger's sweetheart," Pinkerton said, shaking his head at the wonder of it all. He knew love was a powerful force, he had never really appreciated just how powerful it could be in some men's hearts.

"And the *piece de resistance*, Leroy had you deliver a message to Cole Younger verbatim and when he heard it, he understood what it meant. Cole then broke a leather strap he had hung around his neck that held a diamond wedding ring and gave you the ring to give to Leroy, so Leroy could give the ring to his bride. The word for word verbal message and the diamond wedding ring indeed add an odd twist to an already unbelievable story. The beauty of it is, no one would believe it, even if the story got out," Pinkerton added with a chuckle as he walked over and made two more bourbons with branch water. Sitting Jack's fresh drink down on the side table, he asked, "The ring, do you have it with you?"

Jack unbuttoned his shirt pocket, took out the ring, and handed it to Pinkerton. What met Pinkerton's eyes was a flawlessly cut two-carat diamond nested in an intricately crafted lattice setting, perched atop an exquisite platinum and gold wedding band. The ring was beyond words. The diamond's color, clarity, and precisely-cut facets sparkled in the sunlight coming in through the window, sending out rainbows in every direction.

It was the most beautiful stone Pinkerton had ever seen. He knew its value must be in the thousands. Tipping the ring on its side he read the engraved inscription out loud, "Two Hearts Beating as One."

"Yes, those are the words Leroy asked me to say to Cole. Discovering them engraved into the band of the ring was very strange," Jack said, still puzzled by how these two men had come to hold this same sentiment and to know the other man felt the same way about the same woman.

"Yes, real life is sometimes stranger than fiction, my friend, it surely is," Pinkerton said, as though speaking a self-evident truth.

Pinkerton thought he knew what no one knew, including Jack. He knew Leroy Thompson was William Barton of Lizard Creek, Iowa and that Mr. Barton had three good reasons and a fourth one on the way for seeing to it Cole Younger was either killed or locked up. The wedding ring and the engraved sentiment was a peculiar twist in the tale that was a mystery even to Pinkerton, but then Pinkerton figured not even the keeper of all secrets can possibly know every one of them. This thought brought a broad Cheshire cat grin back to his face.

Seeing his boss's face light up again, Jack added, "There is just one further twist in this tale. Before boarding the train in Mankato, I had the chance to talk to Sheriff Bob Butts, Doc Masters, and several of the sheriff's deputies. Their version of events was very enlightening . . ."

As Allan Pinkerton listened to what Jack had learned in Mankato, he had to admit Jack's revelation that Leroy Thompson was in fact William Barton of Lizard Creek, Iowa confirmed another undeniable truth. It's damn tough to keep a secret, no matter how hard you try. Jack's story also reminded him that Bill Barton still had some work to do, if he wanted to be rid of his alter ego Leroy Thompson once and for all.

In coming days, Jack Philips was relieved to have been taken off the James-Younger Gang case and that all files and notes pertaining to the case had been turned over to the agency and burnt with all other references. For Jack, the ashes of the past ten years provided a sturdy foundation for a new life for him, his wife, and their future children at the Pinkerton National Detective Agency headquarters in Chicago. His reassignment and promotion had been confirmed by President Allan J. Pinkerton himself.

October 1, 1876

Lizard Creek, Webster County, Iowa

Full Circle

IT HAD BEEN THREE weeks since the showdown in Northfield. Bill couldn't help constantly scanning the horizon and habitually looking over his shoulder as he waited day after day for word about the fate of the James-Younger Gang. Bill's nerves were on edge and he became increasing concerned that the gang had escaped what newspapers had come to call the largest manhunt in US history. Bill's list of chores shortened day by day as he tried to burn up his nervous energy by launching into and completing one task after another.

When he heard a horse approaching fast, he looked up from the fence post he was repairing and instinctively jumped for his rifle until he saw it was Wilber coming on horseback, hell-bent for leather across the stubble of his recently harvested cornfield.

"Bill, Bill, you won't believe it!" Wilber cried out as he reined up his horse and jumped off. He ran over to Bill and handed him a copy of the Fort Dodge *Messenger,* dated September 28, that told of the gunfight outside of Madelia, Minnesota that had resulted in the death of Charlie Pitts and the capture of Cole Younger and his brothers, Jim and Bob. The article went on to report that the James brothers were last heard of in Sioux City, Iowa where they waylaid a Dr. Mosher and took his clothes and horses. Most now believed that Jesse and Frank James had made a successful escape back to Missouri.

It had been a long wait, but finally the waiting was over. He finally knew which branch in that fork in the road he and Lucy would now be able to travel and in safety. Bill was both relieved and elated. With the Younger brothers locked up in jail and the James brothers back in Missouri, Leroy Thompson was a free man. Free enough to die and be buried for good.

Lucy was so overjoyed when she heard the news, she immediately wrote a letter to Pappy telling him the nightmare was finally over. Wilber waited to take the letter back to Nancy so she could help in sending the good news through her cousin in northwestern Missouri who had helped for so many years to pass messages back and forth between Lucy and her father. Considering all the stories Lucy had shared about Pappy over the years, everyone now looked forward to finally being able meet him.

A week quickly passed since Wilber brought the good news that the Younger brothers had been captured. Pappy and Lucy, finally able to communicate directly, had made up for lost time by exchanging long letters. After so many years of anxious days and nights, it took time for it to sink in that the ever-present threat Cole Younger and his brothers had posed was finally over. The plan now was for Pappy to come up to Lizard Creek for Bill and Lucy's long-postponed wedding right after the baby was born. Johnny and Alda couldn't wait to meet their grandpa.

Just as Bill started to look to the future and put the past behind him, Mankato Sheriff Bob Butts rode into his yard. Bob had promised to drop by when he came down for his duck hunting outing in early October. Bill hadn't expected to see him on his doorstep, however.

Lucy invited him in, and the sheriff recounted the debt of gratitude the town of Mankato owed to Bill for his warning which also helped in Northfield and in eventually bringing an end to the James-Younger Gang. After socializing most of the afternoon, Bob had to be on his way. During their conversation Bill and Lucy shared that they were finally going to have a church wedding after the baby was born. Bob said he was happy the Barton clan was growing, and that Bill Barton was finally going to do the right thing and make an honest woman out of Lucy. Everyone had a good laugh.

Right after Bob mounted his horse, he reached into his saddlebag and handed Bill a wax sealed envelope that seemed to contain something more than a letter.

"I received this U.S. Department of Justice letter by special courier a little over a week ago," Bob said. "It seems they wanted to get this to you and asked me to bring it down here personally. Sorry for not giving it to you when I arrived; however, my instructions were that I should give this to you just before leaving your place after my visit," Bob continued with a confused look on his face. "I hope it's good news," he added as he turned his horse and trotted out of the yard.

Sheriff Bob Butts was more than a little perplexed by the unusual request that had come directly from the Department of Justice by special courier just the week before. He wondered, when he received the wax sealed envelope, why he had been chosen to personally deliver it to Bill Barton. He also wondered how anyone in the Department of Justice would know that he knew Bill Barton and that he would be visiting Lizard Creek at this time of year. The recent events surrounding the demise of the James-Younger Gang had been widely reported; however, no one outside of a handful of deputies and Doc Masters knew Bill Barton had ever been to Mankato or played any role in the demise of the James-Younger Gang.

Unknown to Sheriff Butts, Allan Pinkerton had Jack Philips to thank for these details. Jack had taken the train from Mankato on his journey to Chicago after the capture of the Youngers. Before the train departed, he had a series of chats with Sheriff Butts, some of his deputies and Doc Masters. In those conversations Jack had learned all about the role played by a local farmer from Lizard Creek, Iowa, in warning Mankato of the James-Younger Gang's plans to hit their bank. That same farmer had also warned that if the gang didn't hit Mankato, Northfield was their second choice. The farmer claimed to have overheard this vital information after a chance encounter with the gang that resulted in a life-or-death chase all over northern Iowa. That gentleman farmer had been none other than Bill Barton of Lizard Creek, Webster County, Iowa. That Leroy Thompson, a well-known southern rogue, was in truth Bill Barton, gentleman Iowa farmer, came as one hell of a revelation to Jack Philips.

After hearing Jack's story, Pinkerton immediately saw the opportunity of using Sheriff Bob Butts' trip to Fort Dodge to deliver a final message to Leroy Thompson. Allan J. Pinkerton had also quickly reminded Jack Philips that though his revelation about Leroy Thompson might be interesting, it contained just the kind of conflicting facts that would be best forgotten and buried in his new position at the Pinkerton National Detective Agency. Without protest, Jack had agreed to never speak of the matter again.

Bill stood with a confused look on his face as he turned the envelope over in his hands several times, looking first at one side and then the other.

"What is it, Bill?" Lucy said, interested in seeing what was inside the mysterious wax-sealed envelope.

"Very strange that Sheriff Butts was asked to wait to give this to us until he left," Bill said, trying to figure out the meaning of the strange request for the delivery of the wax-sealed envelope. "It seems that someone at the Department of Justice didn't want the sheriff or anyone else to know what was in the envelope," he added.

"Well, open it up and let's take a look," Lucy said, anxious to learn what could be so important.

"Alright, let's take a look then," Bill said, shrugging his shoulders as he broke the wax seal and pulled out a folded letter. In the envelope, there was also a hard-folded piece of paper with another wax seal which Bill handed to Lucy.

Bill read the letter out loud,

> Enclosed is a token of appreciation for the information and assistance you provided regarding recent events. I am sure Lucy will love it. Give my regards to Leroy. Please tell him, his job is done once Theodor is taken care of, thirteen should do it. Many happy returns on your upcoming wedding.

> With sincerest regards and best wishes, Allan J. Pinkerton,
> Director, Internal Investigating Unit, U.S. Department of Justice

When Bill finished reading, Lucy, with a confused look on her face, broke the wax seal on the folded paper she held in her hand. Slowly she unfolded the paper, discovering a dazzling two-carat diamond wedding ring tucked inside. "Oh my God! It's so beautiful! Who, how, what does it mean?" Lucy said, confused, surprised, elated all at the same time.

"Look at the engraving on the inside of the band," Bill said, hoping to head off her curiosity about the many revelations contained in the letter. He knew she deserved to know the truth about his outlaw past, he just had never figured out how and when to tell her. At least, that was the excuse he had always told himself.

"It says: "Two Hearts Beating as One." Oh darling, it's wonderful," she screeched, wrapping her arms around his neck and giving him a big kiss on the mouth. Bill liked the direction things were going and was pleased Lucy seemed to have no questions concerning the troubling revelations contained in the letter. Just as they turned to enter the house, Lucy's water broke.

Things moved quickly after that. Bill sent Johnny over to Wilber's place to fetch his wife, Nancy. Nancy was the area's best midwife since she knew a lot about childbearing, having had ten kids of her own. Bill also sent little Alda to fetch water. After helping Lucy into bed, he fired up the cookstove with kindling. After five hours of labor, their second son was born.

"Oh, Lucy. It's a boy and he's been born with a veil!" Nancy cried. "What good fortune. He'll be a man of great wealth and distinction," she said with a degree of awe in her voice.

Babies born en caul are very rare. Such births with amniotic membrane still covering the head or even the whole child at birth have been believed to be auspicious in many cultures around the world down through the ages.

Bill was walking on air. "His name will be Benjamin Bingham Barton, named for his grandfather Oromal Bingham Barton and Benjamin Franklin," Bill said with conviction. Bill wanted the boy to carve out new frontiers in science and discovery and now believed more than ever that, having been born with a veil, the boy would indeed do so.

Bill still couldn't get the thought of Alexander Graham Bell's invention of the telephone out of his mind. He couldn't help dreaming about all the ways this wonderous invention would reshape the future of the world. He had high ambitions for all his children. For his sons, his ambition was that John tame and settle the west and Benjamin become an inventor and captain of industry. For Alda, he wished she would pursue her musical talents, as her piano-playing was already better than her teacher's. Most of all, he wished for happiness for all his children and that they be blessed with their own families of strong children who would one day settle the furthest frontiers of the nation. Bill dreamed of having more sons and daughters and of the many possibilities for their futures. He finally understood why Wilber and Nancy wanted a big family. Families build nations, and he wanted the Barton family to make its mark.

Bill sat next to Lucy's bed daydreaming about his children's futures and his future children; with his mind off in his own world, he almost didn't hear Lucy when she asked him to stay with her when Nancy went home to tend to her own household. Still on a high, he assured her he would stay by her side. Before leaving, Nancy said she would take Johnny and Alda back to her place for supper and would return later to bring back some supper for Bill and Lucy. Bill thanked her, and with that, Nancy was off with the children in tow.

After Nancy and the children departed, the house suddenly fell silent. The noises of childbirth and the excitement of the past several hours seemed to pour out of every door and window and into the ether beyond. As little Benjamin lay snuggled to her breast, Lucy reached over to the side table next to the bed and pulled the diamond ring out of a drawer. Bill in all the excitement had forgotten all about the ring or even where it might be. His bigger concern had been whether Lucy would remember all the details in the cryptically-worded letter from Allan J. Pinkerton and all they might mean.

"Now, where were we?" Lucy said, breaking the spell and getting Bill's full attention. "Why would Allan J. Pinkerton, the head of the Pinkerton National Detective Agency and the Director of the Internal Investigating Unit for the U.S. Department of Justice, send anything to you, Bill Barton, to give to me? Especially since this diamond ring fits the description of the one you told me Cole Younger bought for me in Kansas City ten years ago. And who in the hell is Theodor? And thirteen what should take care of what? And most importantly, who the hell is this Leroy character?" she demanded, rattling off one question after another while holding up and shaking the two-carat diamond ring right in front of Bill Barton's nose and looking straight at him for answers.

Caught by surprise, Bill sat up straight and found that his mouth had suddenly forgotten how to speak. He had never seen Lucy's eyes burn more intensely or heard the tone of her voice sound more emphatic. Bill knew it would take some time to explain the answers to her not-so-simple questions. His problem was he had no idea how Allan J. Pinkerton knew Bill Barton and Leroy Thompson were one and the same. As for the ring, he suspected Jack Philips somehow got the diamond ring from Cole Younger after he delivered Leroy's verbal message. Jack then must have given the ring to Pinkerton. How Pinkerton knew the ring was intended for Lucy, Bill could only wonder. He was puzzled how Pinkerton also knew Leroy Thompson had been a cattle rustler and had bilked Mr. Theodor Jeffers and his investors out of $13,000. He wasn't surprised, however, that Pinkerton wanted Leroy Thompson to stay dead and buried, considering what Jack had said about the Pinkerton National Detective Agency wanting to stay in the shadows concerning the demise of the James-Younger Gang.

Bill would need to square things with ol' Theodor. It still tickled him to think of the look that must have been on Jeffers' face when the Pettis County sheriff took his cattle off the train in Sedalia. It had been Bill who had anonymously tipped off the rightful owner to check for his cattle on that train. Having decided to give up his outlaw ways, he had wanted to set things right by returning the cattle. He would now have to finish the job by arranging for an anonymous transfer of thirteen thousand dollars to ol' Theodor in the coming weeks. He was sure Mr. Theodor Jeffers and his investors would be thrilled. Bill knew he would still have more than plenty of money left over to help his children continue the Barton family march west.

Thinking about how things turned out, Bill felt fortunate in many ways. He couldn't help but feel a little vulnerable concerning Pinkerton's knowledge of his past as Leroy Thompson. He was delighted that Pinkerton had taken pains to assure him that his slate would be wiped clean, as soon as Leroy paid off his debt to Mr. Theodor Jeffers. Once this was taken care of, Leroy Thompson would need to once again die, be buried, and God willing, never be resurrected again.

Looking on the bright side, now that Benjamin had arrived and the Youngers were out of the way, there was no reason to hold up his and Lucy's long-delayed church wedding. He also looked forward to finally meeting Pappy. It would be good to have their children get to know their only living grandparent. Indeed, he hoped Pappy might even come to live with them, once everything settled down. Families needed to know their roots. Pappy had much to share.

As far as Bill was concerned, what made things even better was he now had a dazzling two-carat diamond wedding ring with proper engraving and no longer needed to worry about buying one. His only problem was the bride-to-be. He wondered if she would still have him, once she knew the answers to her questions. No longer able to hide behind endless excuses, he found himself surprisingly relieved to finally be able to tell Lucy the truth about his outlaw past. Explaining everything wouldn't be easy, but he was sure he could do so.

His confidence resided in his certainty that they had both felt and heard the birth of a new sound on that day in the middle of the Little Platte River, the rhythmic sound of two hearts beating as one. If they both held onto that undeniable truth, he knew their love would endure forever.

Epilogue

ON APRIL 3, 1882 Jesse James was assassinated by Robert Ford, one of his own gang members, for a $5,000 reward. Frank James was never convicted of any crimes and lived out his life in Missouri until his death in 1915. Of the Younger brothers, John died in a shootout in 1874 and Bob died in prison in 1889. Cole and Jim were paroled from Stillwater Prison in 1901. Jim soon after committed suicide in 1902. Cole Younger, after receiving a pardon, returned to Missouri in 1903 where he lived until his death in 1916.

And what of the Barton family? Well, they continued their journey ever westward into new adventures in the Dakota Territory and beyond.